Joe looked good

She'd forgotten how he could take command of a room by simply walking into it. From the very first time she'd seen him with his shirt off, as he moved into his apartment, she'd always been taken by the sight of the muscles in his chest.

Yeah, he looked good. Then *and* now.

Nina punched the pillow in frustration. The most frightening thing was that as much as he frustrated her and angered her, as much as he could light her fuse with a wise remark, as much as she hated admitting it—

You're still attracted to him.

She was doomed.

And theirs was a marriage that was far from over....

ABOUT THE AUTHOR

A gypsy at heart, Elda Minger has lived throughout
Europe and the United States—including Palm Springs,
where *Wed Again* is set. When she's not writing, she's
usually either gardening, dreaming, fooling around or
at the movies!

Books by Elda Minger

HARLEQUIN AMERICAN ROMANCE

117—SEIZE THE FIRE
133—BACHELOR MOTHER
162—BILLION-DOLLAR BABY
229—NOTHING IN COMMON
314—WEDDING OF THE YEAR
338—SPIKE IS MISSING
469—BRIDE FOR A NIGHT
489—DADDY'S LITTLE DIVIDEND

Elda Minger

WED AGAIN

Harlequin Books

TORONTO • NEW YORK • LONDON
AMSTERDAM • PARIS • SYDNEY • HAMBURG
STOCKHOLM • ATHENS • TOKYO • MILAN
MADRID • WARSAW • BUDAPEST • AUCKLAND

ISBN 0-373-16510-2

WED AGAIN

Copyright © 1993 by Elda Minger.

This edition published by arrangement with Harlequin Enterprises B. V.

® and TM are trademarks of the publisher. Trademarks indicated with ® are registered in the United States Patent and Trademark Office, the Canadian Trade Marks Office and in other countries.

Printed in U.S.A.

Prologue

Arnie Axel wished he was anywhere but Morton's.

The elegant, power restaurant was crowded on this particular Monday night. Anyone who was anyone in the industry commanded a good table.

Hollywood was full of such petty details. Which table you sat at. How late you arrived to your own premiere. Which interviews a star chose to give, and which reporters he or she chose to blow off.

And here he was, in that most dangerous of industries, actually contemplating a plan so bizarre it was giving him a migraine.

He glanced at his watch. Robert Corbin was late again. How like the action-adventure superstar, who had only rose to fame because Arnie had sent him that first phenomenal script to begin with.

Arnie sighed as he took another sip of his gin and tonic. The whole situation was so hopeless, for a moment he thought about getting drunk. Oh, not in this shark tank. No one was going to get a chance to

gossip the next morning about how Arnie Axel, su-
peragent, was losing his grip. He'd drive home to his
house up in the Hollywood Hills, overlooking the
city, and quietly lose himself in a bottle of gin.

The room came imperceptibly alive, and Arnie
knew Robert had arrived. The agent straightened in
his chair, the movement so slight as to be almost un-
noticeable. He watched as the actor of the moment—if you could call an actor who had just been
in one of the all-time stinkeroos on screen this year
the actor of the moment—walked into Morton's as
if he owned the joint.

Within minutes, he was at Arnie's table.

He hadn't weathered this well, Arnie thought,
looking at the bronzed skin, the bright blue eyes, the
thick dark hair. Fear. He could smell it.

Robert was scared. How nice. It gave Arnie an
edge.

The actor didn't waste any time after ordering the
standard mineral water with a wedge of lime.

"They're going to do it?"

Arnie smiled, his instinctive confidence return-
ing.

"Nina's on the way to your house as we speak. Joe
will be following shortly."

Robert frowned, then remained silent as the waiter
placed his drink in front of him, fawning in an almost comical manner.

An unemployed actor, no doubt, Arnie thought. They all were.

Once the waiter had left them alone, Robert returned to the subject at hand.

"Arnie, are you sure—"

He stopped talking as Michael Carson, head of Titan Productions, deliberately walked by their table and stopped to chat.

"Arnie, Robert. How are you?"

Arnie merely nodded, then waited as Michael and Robert exchanged the usual empty pleasantries. He waited because he knew Michael wanted information only he could give him.

He toyed with the idea of making him ask, and decided he would.

"So," Michael said at last, his shrewd gaze taking in Arnie. "I hear Joe and Nina Morrissey are working on a script."

Arnie took a careful sip of his gin and tonic, then set it down.

"Yes, they are."

"This is news. I thought they were divorced."

Arnie shrugged his shoulders as if to say, it matters in this town?

"You know what I'm getting at. I heard it was a rather messy breakup." Michael revealed his interest by pulling out one of the chairs at Arnie's table and sitting down.

"It was. But you don't have to be in love with someone to work with them." Arnie chose his words carefully, knowing that this particular bit of gossip would be all over the city by tomorrow morning. Phones would be ringing off the hook.

A Morrissey script, with Robert Corbin back in the leading role, would net some studio hundreds of millions of dollars. And if there was one thing Hollywood understood and respected above all else, it was making that almighty buck.

"True." Michael paused. "She was a bit high-strung, from what I heard."

Arnie knew when he was being baited. He also knew Hollywood was an old-boy's town, and that town hadn't liked Nina Morrissey any more than she had liked it.

He gambled on telling the truth, knowing Michael would respect him for it in a roundabout way.

"Let's face facts. Neither of them has done well, professionally, without the other. Together, they're magic."

Michael nodded his head, then smiled. It didn't reach his cold, gray eyes. Robert could have been a chunk of wood in the corner for all the attention he was giving him. Most actors were thought of rather contemptuously by the business people in this town. As were the writers.

As was anyone who had an ounce of creativity in their soul.

"I have to hand it to you, Arnie. You did what no one else in this town could do. You got Joe and Nina together again."

They chatted for a few more minutes, then Michael Carson moved on, a killer shark gliding through his own private lagoon.

Arnie took another sip of his drink, then glanced at Robert and smiled reassuringly.

Well, he'd managed to get Joe and Nina Morrissey together again to write a script. But there was only one little missing detail. A crucial detail to this particular deal.

Neither knew the other was involved.

Chapter One

She was running for her life.

The Mercedes skimmed over the highway. Nina Morrissey didn't bother looking at the desert beyond. It was nighttime, the best time for traveling from Los Angeles to Palm Springs. She'd wanted to make the two-hour trip in a relatively calm manner.

She'd wanted time to think about how she was ever going to write this script without Joe.

She'd been so crazy with fear, she'd even thought about tracking him down, calling him, swallowing whatever pride she had left, and simply begging him to come with her to Robert Corbin's lush estate in the hills above Palm Springs.

Which would have been quite a feat, considering that she loved him and hated him all in the same breath.

The deal Arnie had arranged for her had been a godsend. Robert was willing to give her the use of his house in Palm Springs for the next few months, until she could come up with a decent treatment.

Once the hopefully high concept was sold to a major studio, then she could remain at the superstar's estate, use his two pools, his tennis court, his private gym, and have the entire run of the place if she would simply write him an action-adventure script that would put him back up on top.

His last film had not done big business at the box office. So Robert Corbin was scared, because in Hollywood you were only as good as your last picture.

The scripts that she and Joe had written together had made Robert a star. The character they'd created, John Blackheart, had gone on to become one of the best-loved characters in the movies within the last decade. The first three movies in the series had done incredible business both domestically and overseas, and Robert Corbin's star had been firmly placed in the Hollywood firmament.

Then the divorce. Another writer had been brought in to do the fourth John Blackheart script, and the finished film had made a thud that had been heard 'round the world.

Literally.

So Arnie had asked her back, and she had needed this deal, something, in order to pull her life together. In order to help her believe that life could be better.

Without Joe, she added, before she could stop her thoughts.

Nothing had worked since she'd left him. Finances hadn't been that much of a problem, but the rest of her life had gone straight to hell. She'd tried to write without him and completely froze. Total, all-consuming fear. They'd complemented each other in a funny way, come up in the business together, grown as writers together. Each had strengths and weaknesses the other hadn't possessed.

And personally...

She hadn't known the true nature of their relationship, what they'd needed and wanted from each other, until she'd walked out the door.

But she didn't regret leaving him.

Yes, she did.

No, she didn't....

She turned the radio to a jazz station and pressed her foot down more firmly on the accelerator. The last part of the trip, on Interstate 10, was an invitation to speed. The highway was flat and smooth, there was no sound except the soft hum of the heater and the rush of desert wind outside the windows.

Oh, Joe....

This particular job was bringing back painful feelings she'd wanted to forget. Forever.

HE WAS RUNNING on empty, and had been ever since the divorce.

Joe Morrissey was lying on the couch in his West Hollywood apartment, his basset hound, Clyde, at his feet, when the telephone rang. Who would be calling this late at night?

He picked up the receiver.

"Yeah?" He knew his tone was belligerent, and he didn't even care.

"Joe?"

"Arnie."

"How are you?" The question was cautious.

"I've been better."

"I have a job for you."

"Yeah?" He kept his tone cautious, but swung up off the sofa and stretched. Clyde didn't move a muscle.

"How would you like to write the next John Blackheart film for Robert Corbin?"

His body tensed. He'd gone to see the fourth film in the series, and walked out a third of the way through, his guts twisting. He and Nina should have been in the theater, eating popcorn and laughing, making whispered remarks and private little jokes during the dialogue, poking and pinching and kissing and fighting and...

"Joe?"

"What's the deal?" He knew he sounded suspicious, and he didn't even care. Hollywood had beckoned to him with her irresistible siren song, and he'd answered. He'd wanted it all so badly, and it had cost him his career, his marriage, his very soul.

It had cost him Nina, and that had just about killed him.

Briefly, Arnie explained.

"Palm Springs?"

"Haven't you been to his house before?"

"Arnie, you forget. I'm the writer."

"This could be good for you."

He swallowed. *What about Nina?* But he didn't ask. Couldn't. Some things were just too private.

Too painful.

He glanced around the small apartment. There was absolutely nothing about it that made it a home. He simply lived there, existed from day to day as he wondered what he was going to do with the rest of his life.

He'd tried writing alone, but his heart hadn't been in it. He'd missed Nina so badly, and simply sat staring at the computer screen, remembering. . . .

"Joe?"

He tried to read Arnie's emotions over the phone, and couldn't. He was just too tired.

"Yeah, I'll do it." He swallowed hard. "I hated what those bastards did to John Blackheart in the last movie."

Arnie was silent for a moment, then said quietly, "It was a truly awful film."

"Yeah, well, those guys didn't know what they were doing."

"You and Nina should have written it."

I know, Arnie, I know, you don't have to tell me....

"Yeah. I'll leave as soon as I pack a few things. Is it all right if Clyde comes along?"

"I don't see why not...Robert insisted you make yourself totally at home. Now, call me when you get there. And if you have any problems."

"Yeah." Joe hung up the phone and leaned back against the sofa. He could hear the sounds of traffic outside through the partially closed blinds, but he simply closed his eyes and thought about what he had just committed himself to.

You can't do it without her. And you know it.

He could call her. He could try. He opened his eyes and stared at the ceiling.

You could get her back. This is the absolutely perfect excuse.

He could call her and try to be civil and polite, which would be a tough one because he was still furious at her for walking out on him when he'd needed her the most.

The thing was, he still didn't understand why she'd left him. He'd caught up with her, and they'd fought, but nothing had been resolved. Something had gone wrong with their basic ability to communicate with each other.

It was as if he were supposed to read her mind. And if there was one thing Joe Morrissey wasn't good at, it was second-guessing the female mind.

Forget it. You've got work to do.

He had enough natural arrogance to believe he could certainly write a better script than that last disaster he'd seen up on the screen.

But it wouldn't be the same without Nina.

SHE ARRIVED at the compound a little after midnight.

The January desert air was cold and crisp, and the wind was still blowing as Nina reached the small guardhouse. Robert Corbin's Palm Springs home was his sanctuary, the place where he escaped the craziness of Los Angeles.

The house was perched high on one of the mountains overlooking Palm Springs. It had been built into the side of the mountain, with terraced gardens and huge glass windows to let in the strong desert sunshine.

She gave her name to the guard, showed him some identification, then continued her journey up the steep driveway.

Here in the desert, she'd be locked away for the next few weeks, whipping the treatment into shape. She looked forward to the solitude, and hoped it would be healing. Nina wasn't sure of much anymore, but she knew she couldn't continue the way she'd been going.

She had to figure out what to do with the rest of her life, how to fill the void in her life that Joe had left—and the prospect didn't make her happy.

Once the Mercedes was parked in the huge, circular driveway, she stared up at the house and wondered which room inside this massive structure would be hers.

Before she could ponder too long, the immense double door opened and a slightly built Asian man slipped outside. He started toward her car, and she opened the door and got out.

"Miss Morrissey?" His accent was English, his manner impeccably polite.

"Yes."

"My name is Sam. Mr. Corbin asked me to make you welcome."

"Hello, Sam." They shook hands, and she liked him instantly.

"Come inside, please. I'll have the staff see to your bags..."

"I've got some live luggage—"

"Ah, the cats." Sam smiled, and Nina was touched by the happy expression in his dark eyes. "It's been a long time since there have been animals at this house."

"I talked with Robin—"

"No, no. You misunderstand. Of course it's all right, you shouldn't be expected to be separated from them for so long a time."

"I thought..." Nina wrinkled her forehead. "Arnie told me Robert had a dog."

"Oh, yes." Sam seemed slightly discomfited for a moment, then recovered his composure. "We think of Clyde as one of the family, not an animal. He's at the vet's, getting a bath and his nails trimmed. He'll be arriving back at the compound tomorrow."

"And he likes cats?"

"Clyde likes everyone, Miss Morrissey."

"Nina. Please call me Nina."

"As you wish."

Sam was most efficient, and within half an hour, her luggage and three cats were ensconced in one of the most beautiful bedrooms Nina had ever seen.

The wall that overlooked the Coachella Valley was made entirely of glass. She couldn't see much of the view, there were very few lights this late at night. But in the morning it would be glorious, especially at sunrise, with the light reaching to the brown mountains on the far horizon.

The bed was huge, the carpet plush. The large master bathroom off to one side was totally sybaritic, the entire place simply decadent.

She wondered what Joe would have thought of it, then squelched that particular line of thought.

Sam helped her set up a cat box and various food dishes in the bathroom, then she let her three feline friends out of their traveling cases.

Ollie bounded out, a fluffy mess of dark orange-and-white fur, meowing excitedly. He rubbed around her ankles, then begged to be picked up. She did, burying her face in his dense fur. He always smelled like baby powder, and now he gently bit her nose.

She laughed as Stan, a light orange tabby who seemed to have a perpetually worried expression, peered cautiously out of his carrier, then put a tentative paw on the deep carpet.

"It's okay, Stannie."

She'd found the two kittens in the corner of a pet shop, in a small cage. Infested with fleas and ear mites, they'd been a pathetic sight. The young man at the counter had told her that someone had found them playing near a dumpster that morning.

"What are you going to do with them?" she'd asked.

"Ah, we'll think of something."

His tone had not been encouraging.

She'd been in the pet shop buying cat food for Henry, and before she'd left, she'd made up her mind. Stan and Ollie had come home with her that very afternoon, even if the last thing she needed was two kittens.

"What about that one?" Sam asked, indicating the third carrier. It was slightly larger than the rest, and had been considerably heavier.

"He'll come out in a minute."

A soft grumble, a cross between a growl and a moan, issued forth from the plastic cat carrier.

Sam shot her a dubious glance.

Nina merely smiled.

"Come on, Henry, it wasn't that bad a trip."

The same noise sounded, a little louder this time.

Nina set Ollie down, then turned to Sam.

"Watch this."

She snapped open a small, three-ounce can of cat food, and a large white blur came whipping out of the last carrier.

"Hey, Hen, I knew you wouldn't turn down the chance of a meal."

"That's a *cat?*" Sam said, his tone incredulous.

"He is kind of big. But he's on a strict diet." When Sam didn't say anything and merely continued to stare, Nina felt compelled to explain.

"He belongs to my landlord, and I was looking after him while he and his family were in England. When I got this job, I called him and asked him if I could take Henry along. I thought he'd be happier here than at a cage at the vet's."

"Would he have *fit* in a cage?"

Nina laughed. She was used to people's reactions to Henry. Bubba and Mel's feline friend weighed in at twenty-six pounds, and was on a carefully monitored diet for the next year. His goal weight was fourteen pounds, as he was a big-boned cat.

Henry meowed now, and reached for her jean-clad legs with his claws.

"No, Hen! Hold on a sec!"

Within the minute, he was locked in the bathroom, happily gobbling down his measured portion of food. She and Sam placed Stan and Ollie's wet and dry food on a table at the far end of the room. Henry couldn't jump that high, as fat as he was. Thus, the food would be out of his reach.

"Is there anything else you need before I retire for the night?" Sam asked.

"Oh, I don't want to bother you—"

"A cup of tea? Some warm milk?"

"Tea would be lovely."

Sam left silently, and Nina lay back on the bed and contemplated the next few weeks of her life.

Clearly, Sam was here to make her life easier. All she had to do was figure out another spectacular disaster for John Blackheart to fight his way out of.

Easier said than done.

Ollie jumped up on the huge bed, walked over to where she was lying down and climbed up on her chest. He pressed his nose against hers and breathed mackerel breath against her nose.

"God, Ollie! I should have named you fishbreath!"

He meowed happily. Ollie had broken her heart in the cage at the pet store, meowing and clinging to the steel mesh. He'd been totally without pride, everything in his feline body language begging her to take him home.

Stan had been the opposite, sitting quietly. Almost depressed.

She couldn't have taken one without the other, and now they complemented each other in a strange sort of way.

She petted Ollie until Sam returned with her tea. He'd included several small sandwiches and a plate of cookies on the tray, which he now deftly placed on the bedside table.

"If you need anything at all, at any time, simply dial three. It rings through directly to my quarters." He glanced at the bathroom, and Nina knew he was fascinated by Henry. Most people were. The Jackie Gleason of the cat world, Bubba had called him. The Great One.

"Thank you, Sam."

"You're to set your own hours. Whatever helps you to be most creative. I'm usually in the kitchen or the garden, so if you're hungry, I can certainly fix you something."

She nodded her head, then Sam left the room as silently as he'd entered it. Nina poured herself a cup of tea, then picked up one of the delicate sandwiches.

Robert had thought of everything. All the mundane chores were taken care of, leaving her with nothing to do but write the screenplay.

She was too tired to be scared. She finished another sandwich, then three of the cookies. Finishing her tea, she let Henry out of the bathroom, changed into a sleepshirt and fell asleep as soon as her head hit the pillow.

"ROBERT HAS three cats?" Joe said, talking to Arnie on his car phone. "I thought he was allergic."

"Oh, you know the things doctors can do with allergies these days. Nothing short of miraculous."

"In a way it'll be good. Clyde will have someone to play with."

"Exactly. And you, my friend, will have plenty of time to create another story." Arnie paused. "Any ideas?"

"Not a one," Joe replied cheerfully. Arnie was a terrific agent, and he'd always been able to be totally honest with the man. "But I'm sure I'll come up with something."

"So you didn't reach Nina, then," Arnie said, changing the subject.

"I called the last number she had listed under her name, but the phone just kept ringing."

"It's her current number. Maybe she's away on vacation and disconnected her machine." Arnie paused again. "Would you have been comfortable working with her, Joe?"

"I don't know. I feel kind of...guilty. John Blackheart was just as much her creation as mine."

"She'd want you to do this, Joe."

"Think so?"

"I'm pretty sure."

"Arnie, can you do me a favor?"

"Certainly."

"Try to reach her. Feel her out, see what she thinks. I think the script would have a better chance of turning out right if both of us worked on it." Joe leaned back, happy that the first step of his master plan was being put into operation. Arnie would never suspect there was an ulterior motive involved.

"I'll do that. Now, drive carefully, and let me know how things work out once you arrive."

"Right." Joe hung up the car phone, then reached over and scratched Clyde behind his long, floppy ears. The basset hound made a low, moaning sound, then promptly went back to sleep.

The Mercedes was steadily eating up the miles between Los Angeles and Palm Springs. He'd be at the compound within forty minutes. Setting the radio to an all-night jazz station, Joe decided to lean back and simply enjoy the ride.

HE ARRIVED at the compound a little after two in the morning. And as he was a night person through and through, the odd hour didn't bother him a bit.

The immense double door opened, and a slightly built Asian man slipped outside.

"Ah, Mr. Morrissey. You made excellent time. Let me help you with your bags."

"No need. I've only got the one." He turned toward the dark gray Mercedes. "Come on, Clyde, up and at 'em."

No response.

He turned toward Sam. "Sometimes he needs a little prodding. Like, some food."

"Ah, yes. Henry is a lot like that."

"Robert with a cat? I still don't get that one."

"Oh, you'd be surprised at the things that go on in this house." And with that rather inscrutable remark, Sam led the way into the house.

His bedroom was incredibly luxurious. He thought of Nina when he saw the bathtub, and remembered all the showers and baths they'd shared.

Get a grip.

Sam brought him a cold beer, then Joe kicked off his boots and stretched out full-length on the king-size bed. He wasn't tired, and reached for the remote control on the bedside table. The bedroom boasted a fifty-inch television set. Joe had to hand it to Robert Corbin, the man thought of everything.

He took a long pull on his beer as he whipped through the various channels, finally settling on an old, black-and-white movie from Hollywood's golden years.

Those guys sure knew how to write 'em.

He settled back, knowing it would be several hours before he'd fall asleep.

SHE WOKE UP at ten, and realized Sam had slipped into her bedroom and pulled the drapes shut. Otherwise, the bright desert sunlight would have disturbed her deep sleep. He'd also fed the cats, as their hunger would have had the same results.

Nina headed toward the bathroom, then stepped into the huge shower stall. She'd spray herself awake. Most mornings it was hard to get going, partly because she hadn't felt truly healthy in a long, long time.

Last July, she'd contracted pneumonia and spent the better part of the year under the weather. The only person she'd confided in was Arnie, and she'd sworn him to secrecy. Rumors about a writer's health could ruin a perfectly good career.

And hers wasn't even perfectly good.

The only reason she'd stayed out of the hospital was that she'd begged her doctor to let her recuperate at home. Strict bed rest had been her physician's prescription, and Nina had retreated to her bedroom. Thank God for cable TV, or she would have gone out of her mind with boredom. She hadn't even possessed the energy to pick up a good book.

She'd watched movie after movie, but only when the first movie she and Joe had scripted together, *Deadly Threat,* had come on, had she allowed herself to cry for all she and Joe had lost.

Nina stopped midshower, and let the hot water pound down over her tense shoulders as she remembered. It wasn't even the death of her career that had meant so much. The death of their relationship had been far more painful.

Looking back, she wasn't even sure what had happened. There had been weeks, months of silent frustration on her part, then a final fight before she'd walked out the door. The strange thing was, she'd thought at the time that she would feel much better simply leaving Joe.

Now she knew better. Now she knew that there would be a part of her that would stay frozen forever without him.

It hadn't been the ordinary relationship. They had been friends for the longest time, before any romance had developed. Then they had been each other's champions, then partners, then semicelebrities.

Then the roller coaster of fame had gone completely out of control.

Nina finished washing her hair, then stepped out of the shower. All three cats were inside the bathroom. Stanley was playing with a tendril of steam, Henry was lying on his back on the plush throw rug and Ollie was sitting in the sink.

All three were patiently waiting for her. Her little family.

"All right." She rummaged through her tote bag until she found Ollie's baby brush, then began to run the short white bristles through his fluffy fur. Though she brushed him every day, Ollie never looked completely groomed. Now he purred loudly and leaned into the brush.

Henry meowed hopefully.

"Can't fool me, Hen. I know Sam fed you."

Henry, disgruntled, padded over to one of the corners of the bathroom and lay down.

Once she finished brushing Ollie, Nina reached for a towel and began to dry her hair.

Ollie meowed, the sound plaintive and heartrending.

"Q-Tip. I know."

She dug into the tote again, and produced the swab for the cat, who promptly grabbed it between his teeth and hopped off the sink. He thundered out of the bathroom, Stanley in his wake.

Nina smiled as she watched her kittens go. Though they were both almost a year old, they'd always be "the kittens" to her.

Now, as she toweled herself dry and stepped into clean underwear, she thought about the day ahead.

Breakfast, then a short morning stroll in the garden and some breathing exercises. Then she'd sit out in one of the hammocks by the outdoor pool and see what her subconscious mind could come up with in the way of suitable tortures for John Blackheart.

At the mere mention of the character's name, she thought of Joe. Why hadn't Arnie asked him to write the script?

It didn't seem right, going on without Joe.

She wondered what he would do when he found out.

Within the hour, she'd eaten one of Sam's spectacular cheese-and-spinach omelets, downed a glass of fresh-squeezed orange juice, done her breathing exercises and was lying in a hammock in the shade, notepad in hand.

SOMEONE WAS tickling his nose.

"Nina, stop," he said softly, his mind still dreaming of happier times.

The tickling continued.

"Nina..."

Something cold and wet hit his right cheek.

Joe opened his eyes and stared into golden feline eyes. A cat was sitting on his chest, happily shredding the fluffy tips of a cotton swab.

"You must be Ollie," he said, his voice gravelly.

The cat meowed happily, then spit out another piece of cotton. This time it landed on his nose. Joe wiped it away, then grabbed the Q-Tip out of Ollie's mouth. A short game ensued, until he tossed it over the side of the bed and the cat raced after it.

He swung his legs over the side of the bed, then stretched. Glancing at the clock, he realized he'd slept through the morning. Twelve thirty-three. Well, he'd always been a night owl, and besides, there had been some great old movies on last night.

Pulling on a pair of well-worn jeans, he ambled down the long hallway in what he hoped was the direction of the kitchen. Sam was there, busily chopping vegetables. Sitting at the man's feet, Clyde looked up hopefully.

"I hope you like dogs," Joe remarked, pouring himself a cup of coffee from the pot on the kitchen counter. "Where there's food, there's Clyde."

"He's no problem. What would you like for breakfast?"

"Actually, I was hoping you could tell me where the pool was."

"Indoor or outdoor?"

Joe grinned. He'd really fallen into it this time.

"Indoor."

"I'll escort you there. If you'd like, I could bring you breakfast after your swim."

Joe hesitated, then realized that the houseman was eager to please his employee's guest.

"That would be fine. In about thirty minutes."

Once in the Olympic-size pool, he swam laps furiously, wondering how he was going to write the latest installment of John Blackheart's adventures without Nina by his side.

He still wasn't sure exactly what happened when they worked together. All he knew was that it was magical. They complemented each other in a crazy sort of way. She steadied him, gave him a certain balance, and a much calmer perspective.

He walked up out of the shallow end of the pool and reached for his terry-cloth robe just as Sam came in with his breakfast tray. Clyde was at his heels, his long tail wagging hopefully.

"I've already taken the liberty of feeding your dog, sir...."

"Joe."

"Joe. Otherwise, I was afraid he might have disturbed your sleep."

"I appreciate it."

Sam settled him at a table by the far end of the pool, then glided out as discreetly as he'd entered the large, glass room. After tossing the basset a chunk of a banana nut muffin, Joe dug into his omelet.

Robert Corbin didn't fool around. But Joe wasn't fooled by the superstar's generosity. Robert's last picture had bombed big, and the actor was desperate. So desperate that he was giving Joe the run of his house.

I could get used to this, he thought as he took another sip of coffee. *Too bad Nina can't see all of it.*

He had to get her out of his mind. He had to get to work, and prove to himself he could handle this assignment. Arnie had a lot of faith in him, and he couldn't let his agent down.

He'd brought a black felt-tip pen and yellow legal pad out to the pool with him. Once he finished his breakfast, Joe poured himself one last cup of coffee, picked up his pen and resolutely got to work.

Chapter Two

Life-styles of the Rich and Famous wasn't all that bad.

Nina had spent the day lying by the pool. Even though she'd been covered in sunscreen and had a bandanna tied over her hair, she knew she'd gotten a little color.

The mountains had looked gorgeous in the distance, the air had been healing, fresh and clean, warm with the faintest scent of desert vegetation. Bright sunlight had been rejuvenating, and she could understand why people moved to Palm Springs for their health.

She'd sat outside for almost six hours straight, with short breaks for the bathroom and refreshments.

And she'd written down exactly five ideas. In retrospect, all of them stunk.

The day had been a complete waste. Now, after dinner, panic was beginning to set in.

She lay in bed, the drapes drawn, all three cats on the king-size mattress with her.

Her gaze strayed to the phone.

Call Arnie. Tell him you can't do this.

But her hand didn't move.

Call him tomorrow. You may as well get a good night's sleep.

She missed working with Joe. Missed their arguments, the way they made each other justify their ideas, prove to each other why and how a particular idea was the best possible direction the script could take. Whenever Joe had given her that look that told her he thought her idea was crazy, she'd been more determined and stubborn than ever to make him see it was the right move.

The silence by the pool had been deafening.

She rolled over and buried her face in the pillow, hiding from the world. She'd call Arnie and admit defeat tomorrow. Tomorrow would be soon enough.

JOE WAS an honest writer, and he was nothing if not honest about a day's production.

Today's work had reached an all-time low. He'd known when he'd fallen asleep by the indoor pool and had that same dream.

He was in a car with John Blackheart, racing down Mulholland Drive. The sports car had been hugging the turning and twisting mountain road, then veered off down a hill, where it crashed with a satisfyingly blazing explosion.

He'd woken with a start, then glanced around, his heart pounding. All had been quiet by the pool, Clyde snoring softly by his side.

Some dream.

You didn't need Freud to figure that one out.

It was the old crash-and-burn.

Now, lying in bed, he wondered how he was going to write a decent script. It wasn't fair to Arnie, being here if he couldn't deliver the goods. It certainly wasn't fair to Robert.

He picked up the phone.

Arnie answered on the third ring.

"I can't do it."

"Joe, calm down."

"No, Arnie, listen to me. I'm going to save us both a lot of time and trouble. I'm bowing out now."

"Joe. Listen to me. What would you say if I told you that Nina might be willing to work with you."

"You talked to her?"

"In a manner of speaking."

"Arnie, don't start prevaricating. What are you getting at?"

"I think the two of you need to work together again."

"Okay. Okay. Fair enough. I could go for this."

"Do you think you could both behave like civilized adults?"

"Of course. This is work, you know?"

"Hmm. Well. I'll talk to her this evening, then get back to you."

"Okay, Arnie, but try to make it fast. I can't stay in this place in good conscience knowing I can't pull this project off."

"I'll call you this evening."

THE PHONE RANG in Nina's bedroom and she picked up.

"Nina, my dear, how are you?"

"Fine, Arnie." She paused, hating herself for lying to him. He didn't deserve it. Arnie had never been anything but fair and square with her.

"Actually, not so fine."

"Is there anything I can do?"

"I think you should let Joe handle this project. Arnie, I...I can't do it. I'll be leaving in the morning."

"Oh, Nina."

"I'm sorry I let you down—"

"What if I told you I'd talked to Joe and he'd offered to work with you?"

The thought silenced her. Totally.

"Nina? Are you still there?"

"Yes." She paused, considering.

"Would it be so terrible?"

She wondered if she could face seeing Joe again. What it would be like to work with him. If she could even stand to be in the same room with him.

And in a way that only another writer could understand, she wondered if she could let John Blackheart die with that horrible last movie as his final exit.

"Nina?"

"Arnie?" she said shakily, trying to get her breathing under control and not sound like she was wheezing. "Could I have tonight to think about it and call you in the morning?"

"Certainly. I'll be in the office all day."

"Thanks. I appreciate it."

After she hung up, Nina rolled over and stared at the ceiling. And wondered how her life could have gone so very wrong.

WHEN A SCREENWRITER is in the pits, the only sure cure is to go to the movies. Or in this case, stroll down the hall to Robert Corbin's state-of-the-art screening room, where an enormous big-screen TV awaited, along with a sound system that would put most movie theaters to shame.

So thought Joe, as he stepped out of the shower after a satisfying dinner. Sam had outdone himself with a shrimp stir-fry, and now he was ready for some mindless entertainment before the big decision tomorrow.

He wondered about working with Nina again. In his most vengeful fantasies, he'd thought of her home, alone, in a crummy apartment, watching the Academy Awards while he walked confidently up on stage and took the Oscar for best original screenplay out of Michelle Pfeiffer's beautiful hands.

Watching while he thanked everyone who had helped him in his entire writing career, while very pointedly leaving her out.

Childish. Foolish. But deeply satisfying on a totally immature level.

Tonight was a night for total immaturity. Sam was fixing a huge bowl of popcorn, with Clyde probably close to his side. The dog never moved, unless there was a possibility that some food might come out of it.

Popcorn with real butter, a huge cola—easy ice— a comfortable sofa, a big-screen TV—

And thou . . .

He couldn't stop missing her. And if he were honest with himself, after he'd done the obligatory thanking the Academy, and the producer, director and all the other must-thanks, he would have thanked Nina for opening him up in such a way that his best writing had been possible.

Maybe she'll want to work with you.

Yeah, and maybe the Coachella Valley would suffer an earthquake of around 9.0 on the Richter scale, and the earth would open up and swallow him, and his troubles will be over....

But now wasn't the time to worry. Tomorrow would be soon enough. Now, his hair longish and in need of a trim, and clad in only a pair of faded jeans, Joe stepped out of his bedroom and ambled down the hall toward the lavish entertainment center.

NINA HAD DECIDED to do what screenwriters have done from the beginning of time when their projects were going down the tubes. A movie marathon.

And Robert had every movie known to mankind in his state-of-the-art entertainment center. Sam, after outdoing himself with a spectacular shrimp dinner, was making a huge bowl of popcorn. She'd already requested a cola with plenty of ice and a package of malted-milk balls.

She wondered about working with Joe again. In her most vengeful fantasies, she'd thought of him at home, in some crummy apartment, watching the Academy Awards while she swept confidently up on stage and took the Oscar for best original screenplay out of Mel Gibson's gorgeous hands.

Watching while she thanked everyone who had helped her in her entire writing career, while very pointedly leaving Joe out.

Childish. Even foolish. But so deeply satisfying on a totally immature level.

Well, tonight was a night for total immaturity. She'd curl up on the huge black leather sofa in the entertainment center, the cats by her side, with cola and candy and real buttered popcorn, and drown herself in about three movies.

And miss Joe....

She couldn't stop missing him. It went deeper than the work, and she knew it. And if she were totally honest with herself, after she'd raced through the obligatory thank-yous, she would have thanked Joe and credited him with helping her win an Oscar, because it had been his daring and courage and optimism that had kept them on track from day one.

Okay, look at the bright side. Maybe he'll want to work with you.

Joe, be rational about work? Joe, be rational about anything? You're forgetting that Latin temper....

But now wasn't the time to worry. Tomorrow, calling Arnie, would be soon enough. Now, dressed only in a long T-shirt, her hair pulled up on top of her head in a makeshift bun, and expensive night cream smeared all over her face, Nina walked quietly out of her bedroom and headed down the hall toward the lavish entertainment center.

THE ROOM WAS already dark, and one of her all-time favorite movies, *An Affair to Remember* with Cary Grant and Deborah Kerr, was just beginning.

How thoughtful of Sam, to have started a movie for her.

She was hopeless with anything mechanical, including her own computer. Showing absolutely no foresight whatsoever, she'd left all that technical stuff up to Joe.

Sexist, but the truth.

Now, she picked out the black leather sofa toward the front of the large room. Full of enthusiasm for a night watching movies, Nina bounded around the corner of the couch and flung herself down into what she thought would have been buttery-soft, leather cushions.

And instead, landed in someone's lap.

That someone stood up, dumping her on her butt, and turned on the lamp by the far side of the sofa.

Glancing up from her undignified position on the floor, Nina felt her face flame and her heart start to pick up speed. She finally understood that phrase from one of the Rambo movies:

"I'm your worst nightmare."

HER worst nightmare was standing right in front of her, looking down at her.

"What are you—"

"How did you—"

Both of them stopped talking simultaneously, then each said, "Arnie!"

"No," Nina said, her voice low and angry as she got up off the floor and dusted her butt off with both hands. "Not again, not in a million years!"

"Hah! The feeling's mutual. I couldn't work with you if my life depended on it!"

"Oh, yeah? Well, I haven't noticed you turning out any stellar work since the divorce!"

"Yeah, well some of us don't have trust funds to depend on."

"Low blow, Joe. Really low. Try to think of something a little less clichéd. I'd expect more from you."

The argument escalated as Clyde quietly hopped up on the couch and buried his long nose in the popcorn bowl. Ollie was right behind him, batting a fluffy kernel along the length of the couch.

Joe reached for the remote and turned off the movie.

"When did you get here?" he demanded.

"Last night. You?"

"Last night, around two."

"Then I was here before you were."

"What are you, pushing for squatter's rights?"

"Joe, get off it. I'm going back to my room and calling Arnie right now. You don't have a thing to worry about, I'm out of here by morning."

"No." He grasped her upper arm, and when she would have pulled away from him, he held on tighter. "*We're* going to call Arnie, right now, from Robert's den, on the speakerphone, and have it out with him.''

"CHILDREN, children, calm down...."

Arnie's voice sounded tired as he listened to both their tirades, their anger at being tricked, their frustration at having to confront each other all over again.

Fortunately, he was a smart enough man, and a clever enough agent, to recognize fear when he heard it.

"Are you both quite finished?"

Nina glanced at Joe, and he glared at her. Both of them turned toward the speakerphone on the huge desk in Robert Corbin's sumptuous study.

"Yeah."

"Okay."

"All right." Arnie paused, and it seemed to Nina he was contemplating his next words with the precision of a master surgeon wielding a scalpel.

When he finally spoke, it hurt almost as much.

"All right. Let's face facts. Neither of you has been burning up the screen since the divorce, and the last John Blackheart movie was an atrocity. Now, you know and I know that the two of you need to work together again, if only to complete one last script and send poor John off into the sunset with the finale he deserves.''

Nina sneaked a peek at Joe, then quickly looked away. She didn't want to risk him seeing her interest. Damn Arnie! He knew the way to a writer's heart was through her work. Watching that last movie had made her so nauseated, she'd had to leave a third of the way through.

"Arnie—" Joe began.

"No. The facts are, your careers have been going down the toilet with a capital T. This is the perfect project to jump-start both of you. Then, once a completed script is in my hands, you can both go your merry ways and never set eyes on each other again."

"It was a dirty trick—" Nina protested.

"Darling, I knew that if either of you realized the other was involved, you wouldn't have shown up. But let me tell you this. Each of you expressed an interest—to me, of course—about working with the other."

Joe shook his head, staring at the far wall.

Nina balled her hands into fists.

"Okay," Joe said finally, after taking a deep breath. "But what if we kill each other before we finish the script?"

"Whatever happened to being civilized adults?"

"That was before I saw her." He glanced at Nina, who glowered at him for talking about her as if she weren't in the room. "I kind of . . . get out of control around her."

"Put it into the work."

"John Blackheart is a hero, not a homicidal maniac," Nina said, pointedly ignoring Joe's frustrated glare.

"You know, Arnie, I could leave tonight," he said tiredly.

"I don't think so, Joe," the disembodied voice said calmly. "Robert has installed a state-of-the-art alarm system that works both ways. Sam has been instructed to turn it on the minute he hears shouting. There's no way you'll be able to leave the compound."

Joe was totally speechless, and Nina felt herself begin to go light-headed.

"Wait a minute," she whispered. "Arnie, I—"

"Nina, I have faith in both of you as far as your work goes, but not as much in your judgment. The alarm will stay on a total of forty-eight hours, and I'll bet money that by the time it's turned off, you two will be willing to work together."

"Arn." This was from Joe. "Remember you asked me if I had any ideas? Well, here's a hot one. John Blackheart is trapped in a luxurious mansion in the hills above Palm Springs with his bitch of an ex-wife. So even though the guards at the towers have automatic rifles and grenades, and the moat's crammed with killer white sharks, he'll do anything to get out."

"Bite me," Nina retorted, then walked out of the room without a backward glance.

BITE ME?

This is something that a mature woman says to her ex when she meets him for the first time after eighteen months?

Bite me?

She lay in bed and contemplated various ways she could make him pay for his remark.

. . . his bitch of an ex-wife. . . .

Oh, Joe, you're going to pay for that one. . . .

Where did he get off blaming everything on her? It had been just as much his fault that their marriage hadn't worked. Maybe even more.

And the worst part of it was, how could she have finally seen Joe after all these months and shown up for their surprise meeting in an old sleepshirt and night cream on her face? Expensive cream, yes, but cream was cream.

I must have looked like a dog.

No, take that back. Clyde looks better than I did.

She'd thought of seeing him again, and, Academy Award fantasies notwithstanding, she'd envisioned herself looking fantastic, glowing with happiness, every visual inch telling him in no uncertain terms she was getting along just fine without him, thank you very much.

So much for that daydream.

Reality was a bummer. That was why she wrote movies.

She'd bet her last dime that Deborah Kerr had never met Cary Grant with night cream on her face.

But then Cary Grant didn't have a phoenix tattooed on his upper right arm. And Cary Grant hadn't grown up the hard way in a tough East Los Angeles neighborhood, with an alcoholic Irish father who'd been a good-for-nothing and walked away, and a Cuban mother who'd held the family together.

Joe looked good. It was pretty clear he hadn't been missing her. She'd forgotten how he could take command of a room by simply walking into it. The first time she'd seen him, he'd had his shirt off. He'd been moving things into his apartment. She'd seen the tattoo, but she'd spent a lot more time looking at the muscles in his chest.

He looked good. Then *and* now.

She punched the pillow in frustration. The most frightening thing was that as much as he frustrated her and angered her, as much as he could light her fuse with a wiseass remark, as much as she hated admitting it—

You're still attracted to him.

She was doomed.

And this was a marriage, in her case at least, that was far from over.

JOE HAD STOPPED by his room just long enough to grab his swimsuit, and now he was swimming furiously up and down the length of the outdoor pool, trying to put Nina out of his mind.

He wasn't even that angry with Arnie, for he knew what his friend and agent was up to. Everything the man had said over the phone was the God's truth. They were useless without each other.

The question was, did Nina feel they were useless divorced, as well?

His reaction to her had excited him, stunned him and finally frustrated him. From the moment he'd first seen her, when she came to welcome him to the apartment building on Sycamore, he'd had a major case of the hots for her.

And Joe Morrissey, who'd never waited for a woman in his entire life, found himself at the beck and call of a delicate little blonde who didn't even realize what was going on.

They'd been friends forever—or so it had seemed to his testosterone-crazed system—but when they'd finally made love, it had been as if the stars had fallen out of the sky.

He'd been a jerk. She'd left him. A part of him had died inside. Should have been end of story.

Fade out.

Fade in. Trapped in a mansion together. He had forty-eight hours to convince her to stay. In a crazy kind of way, Arnie's plan was playing right into his.

Forty-eight hours.

Forty-eight hours to convince the woman he'd never stopped loving that they shouldn't be apart, and forty-eight hours to get past the intense anger and pride that should have demanded he track her down and make amends long before this.

He hauled himself out of the deep end of the pool, panting, gasping for breath. It was the only way he'd be able to sleep in the same house with her, exhausting himself to the point where he could just drop into his bed and pass out.

He'd begin his campaign in the morning.

SHE TOOK a long, hot bath—the door locked—and used the eucalyptus herbal bubble bath that Diedre had recommended to open up her breathing passages.

Stan and Ollie didn't like the smell, so they played quietly with a stuffed mouse in one corner of the large bathroom. Henry stayed by the tub, looking up at her with an empathetic expression on his broad little face.

"This," Nina whispered to him, "is the worst mess I've ever been in." She squeezed hot water out of the large sea sponge over her chest.

Henry meowed softly, in total sympathy. He rolled over on the bath mat and waved his four stubby feet in the air.

"But you guys were all on the couch with him."

Henry merely watched her, his golden eyes little slits.

"He is a nice guy, but..." Tears came to her eyes as she remembered more tender moments, and she angrily brushed them away. "Yeah, they're all nice at one time or another. But it didn't last, and that's that."

Forty-eight hours.

Forty-eight hours to survive inside this compound, and then she could get into her Mercedes and leave. She wondered if Joe had driven his. Robert had given them matching gray Mercedes when *Deadly Threat* had been number one with a bullet at the box office.

They'd laughed and laughed over his generosity, and been genuinely awed. Neither of them had ever owned a nicer car. They'd called each other on their car phones, driven all over Los Angeles and decided they'd finally made it. Big-time. Straight to the moon.

How wrong they'd both been. A screenplay couldn't cuddle up to you in bed. Even an Oscar was no substitute for a living, breathing person who loved and cared for you.

Bite me.

She started to laugh as she remembered the expression on Joe's face when she'd lobbed that one at him. She'd hesitated just long enough to register the stunned look he'd thrown her, then headed out the door.

The interesting thing was, she wasn't the little, scared blonde she'd been when she'd first moved to Hollywood. That girl was long gone. Nina knew she'd existed, but it almost seemed like another lifetime ago.

Joe had loved her then. Or at least lusted after her when they'd first met. She couldn't believe it had been almost ten years ago....

Chapter Three

A woman never forgets the day her first marriage ends.

And that event occurred several months before Nina even met Joe.

She merely had to close her eyes to see it all, the memories were that vivid. They had been eating outside, at a small Italian café by the ocean just south of Rome. She'd been married to Brad for almost six months, and had no idea she was so unhappy until that particular moment.

They'd gone to see a film, a romantic comedy. The premise had been adorable, but the ending had fallen down. Over chocolate gelato, she'd been thinking of how it could have been different, and when a lull in the conversation presented itself, she jumped in.

"You know, if I'd been writing that script, I wouldn't have had her come back to him as quickly. I would have changed that part, and I think—"

"Hey! Nina!" Jonathan Trowbridge, Brad's best friend, had interrupted her, snapping his fingers, a smile on his handsome, privileged face. "You know, we really don't give a damn what you think."

There had been six people at the little table, three couples, and everyone but Nina had laughed uproariously. Brad had laughed, too, and she'd been angry when they'd returned to their hotel room that night.

"Why didn't you defend me?" she'd demanded. "He was being a pig."

"Don't be so sensitive, Nina," Brad had replied, fixing himself another drink. "Besides, you were boring. No one wanted to know what you thought. Just leave it alone."

But she couldn't. She didn't understand what was wrong with her, she only knew it horrified her to find out her husband had no desire to really know her. There had never been even the faintest beginnings of true intimacy between them, not the emotional kind.

Something inside her began to go numb, and she couldn't seem to stop it.

Once they returned to their house in London, she decided she didn't want to stay married to Brad. On the surface, what had happened at the café seemed like a small incident, but there had been others.

Brad's verbal abuse was so quick, so clever; he was so blond and good-looking. Simply adorable. He'd been spoiled all his life, and even though Nina's mother had assured her she'd made a good catch, Nina wasn't buying it.

Not anymore.

She broached the subject of divorce with her mother over lunch one afternoon.

Her relationship with her mother was one of the secret sorrows of her young life. Veronica Harte had clearly not wanted children, and Nina had often wondered how she'd been suckered into giving birth to her.

Raised by a succession of nannies, female relatives and mostly by her maternal grandmother, Nina had survived. But she'd never truly flourished in the way a child does when she's assured of a mother's love.

"Divorce?" Her mother's elegant eyebrows had risen slightly, then she'd given her daughter "the look." "Nina, don't be so selfish. You're being ridiculous."

"But he . . . he smothers me."

"And what exactly is it he prevents you from doing?"

"I . . . I don't know. Yet." She couldn't quite locate what her dissatisfaction was, but it was enormous. Nina knew she sounded juvenile, insecure and horribly immature, but she knew with that purest instinct of the heart, her youthful marriage had been a mistake of the first degree.

"This is nonsense." Her mother took a measured sip of expensive white wine, then stared at her daughter in a way that always intimidated Nina. "Everyone makes compromises in marriage, Nina. And you will, as well. You mustn't be so sensitive.''

How strange that her mother should use that word, for she rarely felt anything anymore. But the subject, as far as her mother was concerned, was closed. Nina knew she had been silenced.

Brad had reacted badly when Nina finally gathered her courage and asked him for a divorce, so she'd fallen back into a horrible emotional limbo. She'd spent her days feeling lost and unhappy, in a frozen wordless state.

Until the day she saw Brad with Phoebe.

Phoebe Trowbridge was Jonathan's wife, the man who had made fun of Nina over gelato. She'd seen them through her favorite bookstore's front window, outside on the sidewalk one night. Their arms had been tightly locked around each other, his blond head bent over her darker one.

Nina had been browsing, and the pile of books she'd had in her arms had never made it home. She'd sat down on the staircase at the far back of the shop, then walked unsteadily toward the woman's room where she'd thrown up.

She'd confronted her young husband, and he'd waved off her concerns with the same bored indifference he'd shown toward her other feelings.

"And what if I do see her once in a while? Jon doesn't mind. At least she's not cold to me like you are.''

Somehow it had all become her fault. But this time, he'd committed an indiscretion she could not ignore.

Her grandmother had died when she was sixteen, and for all intents and purposes Nina had lost the only true mother she'd ever known two years ago that night. She had also been left a sizable trust fund that became available on her eighteenth birthday.

Within a week after seeing her husband with another woman, she had gone into the bank and had the entire trust transferred to a bank in Beverly Hills. It was a substantial amount of money, and would easily support her until she decided what she was going to do.

As there was nothing left for her in London, Nina suddenly felt she had the entire world stretched out in front of her. She loved movies, and had always wanted to see where they were made. A few months away was what she needed. This long vacation, away from everyone and everything familiar, made sense. She needed some time alone to sort things out.

Nina was determined she was going to get out from under her mother's thumb, and Brad's, and anyone else's who she sensed didn't truly care for her or even want her around.

She packed two large suitcases and three boxes of books, sending the books on ahead to the postal box she rented over the phone.

The night she left, Brad came home early. They fought and he slapped her, venting his frustration and humiliation in physical violence. She left—simple as that—dragging her cases behind her, sure he thought she only meant to go stay with a friend.

Instead, airline ticket in her purse, she boarded a plane at Heathrow bound for LAX.

On the flight, she caught one of the attendants staring at her, and realized Brad's slap must have left a mark. Taking out her compact, she covered the fresh bruise with a generous amount of makeup, and resolved to cover her tracks from both mother and husband just as carefully.

At first, Los Angeles frightened her.

For almost three days, she stayed at the Hyatt by the airport. She paid cash for everything, and registered in the hotel under a false name.

Brad probably wouldn't come after her, but she couldn't be sure.

On the third day, she took a taxi into Hollywood.

And became enchanted. It was dirty and run-down in places but it was still a town where people believed dreams could come true. She had the cabdriver drop her off in front of Graumann's Chinese Theater, and she wandered about, looking at the stars' footprints and handprints immortalized in concrete.

After coffee and a croissant at a nearby café, she explored the shabby little neighborhood until she found herself in front of a large Spanish-style apartment building with a huge, shaded inner courtyard.

The sign in the front window advertised an apartment for rent. Without any idea she had wanted to do this all along, Nina walked quickly up the front stairs and pressed the buzzer before she lost her nerve.

Walter, the manager, was in his late-twenties, tall and blond and totally outrageous. His ear was pierced in five places, and he had a generous streak of fuchsia hair among the golden blond.

He also knew a lost soul when he saw one.

He showed her the apartment, safe up on the second floor.

It was a studio, one large room with a huge bathroom. The only room for a kitchen was the small area between the main room and the bathroom next to the large closet. He could get her a small refrigerator, bar-size, but it wasn't really the sort of place for anyone who liked to cook.

She didn't even know how.

She paid cash for first and last, then took a taxi back to the Hyatt to get her belongings. Walter came with her, intrigued by what he called her "air of mystery," and helped her move in.

Since her grandmother had died, she'd been lonely. She'd dreamed of her every night. Nothing special, just her life, but her grandmother had always been a part of it, sitting at the kitchen table or working out in the garden. Talking with her. Still there.

Now, with the beginnings of one friendship, she felt a little less lonely.

Nina slept on the ratty sofa in her studio the first night, with blankets and pillows borrowed from Walter. She bought a bed, linens and bath towels the following day. Walter took her under his generous wing, as she found out he had with so many of his tenants, and accompanied her to flea markets, book sales, movies, brunches, and even a few of the parties his equally outrageous friends threw from time to time.

She still had no idea what she wanted to do, but she could finally breathe. She bought books on acting, directing, screenwriting, the history of the movie industry, the art of makeup, anything and everything she could get her hands on.

She felt as if she had been empty for such a long time, and as each book was added to the three oak bookshelves she bought, she could feel that inner, secret, passionate part of herself being filled.

Walter had a friend in Seattle, who sent Nina's mother a telegram worded by Nina. It advised Veronica Harte that her daughter was fine and wanted some time to sort things out—and a divorce.

Several weeks passed before Nina finally bought a secondhand car, a baby blue Dodge. She drove to Westwood that same afternoon and hired herself a lawyer. They started divorce proceedings.

And then Joe moved in, changing her life forever.

"WHO IS HE?" she asked, standing out on her small balcony. Walter had come over to fix the leak in her shower, she'd offered him a cold beer and now they stood looking down at the man who was carrying an overstuffed chair as if it were a stuffed toy.

"Whoever he is, he's gorgeous," Walter said, his eyes never leaving their new tenant's body.

"What's his name?"

"Joe. Joe Morrissey."

Joe Morrissey. She liked the sound of it. Nina had never been so strongly attracted to a man before. Attraction had always built slowly in the past, friendship turning into something more. Brad had been the exception because, after all, her mother had handpicked Brad.

"The welcoming committee!" Walter said suddenly.

She looked at her friend, puzzled.

"It's all right, Britty." That was his nickname for her. Britty for British. Nina had been sheltered growing up, by her stepfather's wealth and her mother's indifference.

It amused Walter, in his gentle way, how little she knew about life in America. Though her mother was French, her father had been born and raised in New England. But she still thought like the girl who had grown up in London.

"It's just a custom, welcoming a new neighbor into the fold. It's too bad neither of us can bake—"

"There's that French pastry shop on Hillhurst—"

Walter eyed the courtyard below. "He's still got a truckload of stuff. If we leave right now, we'll get back in time to welcome him."

THE INSIDE OF Joe's first-floor studio apartment had been a revelation. Books and scripts, piled from floor to ceiling. A fold-out couch for sleeping, and not much more in the way of personal furniture.

But it was his desk that impressed Nina. That and the computer that rested on top of it, along with piles of yellow legal pads and black felt-tip pens.

Joe Morrissey was going to write a screenplay.

How she envied him his confidence, the easy way he announced something that sounded to her as exotic and adventuresome as saying you were going to fly to the moon.

Everything about him seemed larger than life. His warmth, his talent, his style. He was gracious to her and Walter when they arrived on his doorstep with gourmet brownies, and immediately invited them in.

He had a great mane of well-trimmed hair, dark and glossy and thick, pulled back in a ponytail. But it was his eyes that caught and held Nina, then forced her to look away.

Eyes that saw too much, that's what Joe Morrissey had.

She'd never felt these particular reactions to a man before, and not just to his manner of being. He fascinated her, she envied him, she wanted to be like him, so sure and confident and courageous.

I'm going to write a screenplay.

I'm going to set the world on fire.

I've got a creative fire burning in my belly, and I don't care who knows it.

Jonathan Trowbridge wouldn't have dared laugh at Joe. She tried to picture him with the group of friends she and Brad had traveled through Italy with, and the thought made her laugh out loud.

She covered the sound with her hand, then glanced up.

He was watching her, with those dark, liquid, expressive eyes. Eyes that could cause a woman to lose her soul. Bedroom eyes.

On the walk back to her apartment, Walter merely laughed.

"Britty, you've got him if you want him."

His tone was light, his expression kind.

Walter knew almost everything about her. She'd told him all about her past over the meals they'd shared on the run. Walter knew every little hole-in-the-wall with outstanding food in the greater Los Angeles area, and he'd shared them all with her.

He'd helped her survive, because the one daring thing she'd done in her life was getting on that plane. She'd known nothing about the day-to-day hassles of survival in the real world. Walter had never laughed at her, no matter how ignorant her questions, how clumsy her attempts.

His friendship, his being so supportive and non-judgmental, had meant the world to her.

"You think so?"

"Uh-huh."

He dropped her off on her doorstep and waited until she was safely inside before saying, "I'm giving him twenty-four hours. You'll be seeing our Mr. Morrissey again."

IT WAS closer to six.

He came up late that evening, and when she opened the door to his sharp, impatient knock, she caught her breath. He'd been impressive in shorts and no shirt earlier in the day, the sweat running down his hair-roughened chest.

Cleaned up, he was as handsome as sin.

"Dinner?" he asked, cocking his head.

Confident, as well.

She hesitated, and he filled in the silence.

"Because of the brownies," he said, his voice gentler. He was looking at her, really looking, and Nina wasn't sure she wanted him to see too deeply inside.

"I don't know."

"I'll give you my mother's phone number. She'll vouch for me."

She couldn't help smiling at that one, and he pressed further.

"I don't bite."

"I know you don't."

He was waiting for her to make a decision, and she led with her heart.

"Sure."

She took a swift shower, then pulled on the clothing she'd selected so carefully just moments before. Black lace underwear, a pair of faded jeans and a black sweater. She was one of the rare blondes that really looked good in black, and she wanted to look sophisticated tonight.

Black scuffed cowboy boots, the most comfortable footwear she owned, completed her outfit. Then she swiftly brushed her hair out around her shoulders. A touch of makeup and she was out the bathroom door.

He was standing in her living room—her only room—studying the books on her shelves.

"You've read all these?"

"Most of them," she said, striving to keep her voice quiet. Calm. Dispassionate. She didn't want anyone to know how much she cared. Not Joe, not even Walter. She wouldn't risk being laughed at again, even while paying the price of feeling a little dead inside. And so isolated.

"I'm impressed."

She smiled. First date. Best impressions. She barely knew Joe Morrissey, but dinner seemed safe enough.

He had a motorcycle, and she was excited at the thought of hanging on to his waist, zooming off into the night and exploring the city with this fearless man.

He didn't disappoint. He took her to the beach, to a tiny little oceanfront dive Walter would have adored, where they ate some of the best seafood she'd ever had in her life.

They didn't talk much. She didn't want to pry, and she didn't plan on being very forthcoming with details about her own life. She simply wanted to see if she had it in her to enjoy a man's company.

She really enjoyed Joe.

He amazed her. Older than she was by eight years, he was eons older in experience. He'd graduated from high school and joined the service, "seen the world" as he'd put it, then gone right back to college. Now, having graduated with a B.A. in English, he wanted to write.

"How did you know?" she asked. They'd finished dinner, and were having Irish coffee out on the creaky little balcony overlooking the waves.

"I was never one of those kids that wrote poetry and gave it to my mother. And I've never kept a journal in my life. I've just made up stories inside my head for as long as I can remember, and I figured it was time to get it all down on paper. And hope it's interesting."

Me, too, she thought, understanding the silent stories completely. *Me, too.* But she remained silent.

They walked on the beach afterward, and that was when Nina decided she'd go to bed with Joe. She wanted to see what things would be like between the two of them, even though she suspected it would never be a forever relationship.

It wasn't that she was promiscuous. She'd just had so much feeling frozen inside her for so long, she wanted to let some of it out. And she sensed Joe would be kind, and understanding. Gentle and passionate.

She wanted to know.

On the return trip, she leaned into his side, fitting her body against his in a way she hoped conveyed her intentions. She'd never had a place of her own before, and had no idea how to go about seducing Joe Morrissey.

Once they were at her front door, she resorted to one of the oldest lines in the world.

"Would you like to come in for coffee?" she asked.

He looked down at her with such a sweet yet sexy expression in his dark eyes that her heart almost skipped a beat. Nina could feel her face flush as she remembered they'd already had two cups of strong coffee.

Coffee was the last thing on either of their minds.

"Coffee?" he said softly.

She unlocked the door and led him inside.

The room was dark and she didn't bother turning on the light as he shut the door behind them. The large bay window at the far end of the room looked out over the lush, tropical vegetation in the courtyard. The leaves from a banana tree cast patterns on the wall, creating shadows because of outdoor lights Walter had installed.

She couldn't see Joe's face clearly, she wasn't even sure if she wanted to. He was reaching for her, turning her to face him, and all she wanted in the entire world was for Joe to kiss her.

She turned her face up to his, her breath catching softly in the excitement of the moment. Then his arms were around her, their bodies close, and he bent his head to give her what she wanted.

He kissed her as if they had all the time in the world, as if he wanted nothing more than for this moment to go on forever. She clung to his shoulders, feeling the most peculiar excitement course through her. There was none of the awkwardness usually associated with first kisses, and she wondered at the amount of experience he had.

He broke the kiss, pulled her over to the plush couch that took up one entire narrow wall and sat down. She followed him, coming to rest on his lap. Again, his arms were around her, again his lips on hers. Gentle. Searching. As if he didn't want to frighten her.

She wanted to be frightened, before she lost her nerve.

Leaning away from him, she caught the bottom of her sweater in her hands and swiftly pulled it over her head. And heard the sharp intake of his breath when he saw her, clad only in her jeans and a black demi-bra.

"Nina—"

She put her finger against his lips before he could say anything more, then reached down and pulled off her boots. He caught her up against him, hard, and kissed her again. They'd strayed into deeper, more emotional territory. He was older, stronger, and so intensely male. He wasn't going to stop, and that was exactly what she wanted.

His hands shaped her body as he kissed her, as he swiftly unfastened the black bra, unsnapped and un-zipped her jeans. When she felt his fingers curling around the elastic of her black lace panties, she hesi-tated, then took his face in her hands and kissed him back. She tried to put every ounce of feeling, of pas-sion, into that kiss.

It worked.

Once she was naked, he carried her over to the bed, and she watched as he stripped off his clothing, com-pletely unselfconscious in front of her. She studied his body in the shadowed light, curious as to how it dif-fered from her husband's.

She'd only known Brad's touch, and watching Joe, she knew it would be different with him.

Where Brad had been light, Joe was dark. More muscular. He seemed a primitive man, and she sat up on the bed, watching him. She was shocked at the pleasure simply looking at him gave her, but everything about Joe had been different from the start. He was unlike any man she'd ever met in her life, and if she could only have this one night with him, it would be enough.

She wanted someone to awaken her from her emotional deep freeze, and feminine instinct had told her Joe was the man to do it. He looked like the sort of man who knew what to do with a woman once he got her into bed. That first kiss had assured her of that. He felt right, his lips, his tongue, his hands, and now looking at his body, she knew he would be the one to help her past that frozen emotional barrier.

She glanced from his body to his face, and found him watching her, those dark eyes alert. Sensitive to each move she made. She smiled, and reached out her hand, inviting him to her bed.

He hesitated, then reached for his jacket. She watched as he placed the foil-covered packets on the bedside table.

The enormity of what she was about to do engulfed her, and she took a deep breath. He sat down on the bed beside her, touched her cheekbone with his hand, then ran a single finger along the delicate bone.

"What is this about?" he asked, his voice low.

It astounded her, how exquisitely sensitive he was to her mood. And she was suddenly ashamed at the thought of using him. Nina pulled up a corner of the quilted bedspread to wrap around her body, and just as effectively began to shut him out emotionally. Joe remained on the bed, staring at her, his expression intent.

"I don't usually—" she began, then stopped. Of course, that was what any woman would say at a time like this.

They were silent, the only sound the rustle of palm fronds in the wind, the tapping of part of the banana tree against her bathroom window.

She cleared her throat. "You were ... only supposed to be a one-night stand."

"I'm outraged." But his eyes were full of life and humor, and she found herself responding with a smile.

He leaned back against the headboard. He'd adjusted the leg closest to Nina, pulled it up so he looked like an artist's model.

"What was this, some sort of experiment?" he asked.

She swallowed against the sudden, self-conscious tightness in her throat. "In a way."

"What's wrong?"

In the same way she knew he would be good for her sexually, she knew he would listen. And believe her. Slowly, with the tiniest amount of trepidation, she told him bits and pieces of the past.

He didn't say a word, merely listened.

Rain began to fall outside, the sort of Pacific storm that comes down quickly and violently, washing everything clean. Nina leaned back against the headboard, tightly wrapped in the quilt, and continued her story up to the point where she'd seen him moving into the building.

"So I thought—since I'd never reacted to any-one—any *man* the way I reacted to you, it would be a safe bet that sex would be good."

He shook his head, and she saw the beginnings of a smile on his face.

"How old are you?"

"Eighteen."

"Really?"

"Yes."

"And what was sex like with this guy?"

She was never going to see this man again, after what she'd told him. He knew too much, he was emotionally dangerous. She had absolutely nothing to lose, and decided to tell him the truth.

"Pretty bad." She frowned, remembering. "Awful. It didn't seem like he was there."

"And you thought I'd be there?"

"I thought— You excited me just looking at you, so I thought it had to be better. Even a little bit better would still be better."

He laughed then, and slid down in bed until his head rested on the pillow.

"Are you tired?" he asked.

She realized she was exhausted. She felt as if a part of her had cracked open, to spill such intimate secrets out to an almost perfect stranger.

She nodded her head.

"Sleep with me," he invited, and there was no trace of a smile on his face. He was serious. "Sleep with me, just for tonight, and on my honor, nothing will happen."

She contemplated his offer, then realized it had been a long time since she'd felt close to anyone, just that simple closeness of skin to skin and hearing someone breathe.

"You can trust me, Nina."

She liked the way he said her name. She also knew that if she asked him to leave, he would. But most importantly, she felt there was still a lot to be settled between them, and he was giving her the chance to slow their pace and decide where they were going.

"I'd like that."

"Okay."

And in the morning, when she woke, she studied his sleeping face and realized that for the first time in a long time she hadn't dreamed of her grandmother.

She hadn't dreamed at all.

Chapter Four

Joe didn't want to be a one-night stand.

"You were supposed to leave and never call me back," she whispered when he opened his eyes.

He'd smiled, a sexy, lazy smile, full of contentment.

"Not a chance."

They'd talked in bed that first morning, after Nina had brought out croissants and fresh-squeezed orange juice from her non-existent kitchen.

"Where's the coffee?" he'd teased.

"I don't have any."

They learned more about each other. He'd saved up enough money to take six months off and write. She didn't mention her trust fund, but made it sound as if she were planning on going to school.

Truthfully, she had no idea what she wanted to do.

He asked her if she wanted to see him again.

She told him she did.

And then he made another move that changed her life forever. He invited her to his acting class.

"I THOUGHT you wanted to write screenplays."

"I do. But it helps a lot to know where the actor's coming from."

The studio he took her to was in North Hollywood, in a small, nondescript building off Cahuenga. The building smelled old and musty, and was carpeted with a pale, mushroom-colored carpet. Folding chairs were grouped around three sides of the large main room, with the middle left open for exercises and scene work.

Joe's teacher, Geoff Corrigan, was a working actor. She recognized him from a few of the countless movies she'd watched. The older man, with his lion's mane of silvery hair and intense blue eyes, nodded when Joe asked if she could simply sit in and watch a few classes.

They started with warm-up exercises, then several improvisations. Nina could think of nothing more terrifying than getting up on stage in front of other people. Getting up on stage without a script called for courage she simply could not comprehend.

Then the scene work began, and she fell in love.

A tall brunette and a lanky redhead began a scene. Geoff let them play it all the way through, then the two actors sat down on the chairs they'd set up for their scene as they were critiqued. And Nina, so used to being criticized, realized there was such a thing as a helpful critique.

The third scene was Joe's. He'd written it, and acted it with the help of another student. It was a fight scene, two men involved, and the situation was so frightening Nina found herself leaning forward in her seat, clasping her hands tightly together.

Afterward, Geoff seemed pleased.

"Much improved. Do you see how you need to keep cutting dialogue?"

Joe nodded, taking quick notes on a yellow legal pad.

"You have to trust the actor to do his work. It's all in the images, Joseph."

Afterward, he took her to an all-night deli on Ventura Boulevard. A few of his classmates joined them, and Nina felt herself caught up in a warm camaraderie that was similar to what she felt with Walter and his many friends.

But it was different with Joe. In countless, subtle ways, he made it clear she was there with him, they were together, they were a couple.

She didn't mind.

The food was new to her, and she let him order. Matzo ball soup, a pastrami sandwich on rye with hot mustard and cheesecake with cherries on top for dessert.

Afterward, she went back to his apartment with him.

"What did Geoff mean, you need to keep cutting dialogue?"

He rummaged through the wastebasket near his desk, pulling out several sheets of paper.

"The first two times I brought it to class, the scene was too long. Guys don't talk a whole lot when they're getting ready to fight. I know that, I can't tell you how many fights I've seen. But I wrote it—stupidly. Like these guys had all the time in the world to hang around and discuss their feelings."

She studied the pages, instantly understanding the cuts he'd made, realizing how many times he must have worked on this particular scene to get it to play as effectively as it had in Geoff's classroom.

And she knew, at that moment, that he was going to make it.

"Is it part of something else?"

He nodded.

"Can I read it?"

"I thought you'd never ask."

He gave her one of his copies. The script was untitled, but he'd had it professionally covered with black paper and fastened with brass brads. It looked like any of the shooting scripts a person could buy down on the Boulevard.

She sat down on his couch and started to read.

He made coffee.

She turned pages, her face scrunched up in concentration.

He turned on the small television, softly, so as not to disturb her, and watched the news, then a late-night movie.

She finished it exactly two hours after she'd started it, and by that time he'd cleaned up their coffee cups and was ready for bed.

"You like it?" His tone was deceptively casual, but Nina was beginning to read him. His heart was on his sleeve with this one.

"I loved it. How do you know so much about fighting?"

"I've done my share."

"Boxing?"

He nodded.

She remembered the tattoo she'd seen on his right arm, the day he'd moved in. A phoenix, the legendary bird who rose from the ashes of total destruction and recreated itself again and again.

"Gang-fighting?"

"A little. My mother made sure I got out of that as fast as I could, and she was right. It's a dead end."

"Have you ever . . . hurt anyone?"

He took too long to formulate his answer, and she had hers. She set his script down on the scarred coffee table by the couch and crossed her arms in front of her chest.

For the first time, she felt truly uneasy with him.

The silence stretched electrically between them, and Joe finally bridged it. But not with the question she thought he would have asked.

"Did he hit you?"

Joe Morrissey saw too much.

She couldn't answer, simply looked away.

"He hit you."

She nodded.

The word he used in reference to Brad was vulgar, explicit and filled with masculine contempt.

"That's why the post office box, right? And the low profile. You think he's coming after you?"

She pushed her hair out of her face, suddenly tired. Exhausted. "I don't know. I think I probably hurt his pride more than anything else."

She didn't flinch when he touched her face, took her chin in his hand and gently turned her so she had to look at him.

"Why Hollywood?"

"Why not?" Her attempt at lightness failed miserably.

"Come on, Nina," he said softly, stroking her face. "No one moves here just to move here. There's usually a reason. The beach, the industry. You don't just look at a map and pick a town like this one."

She took his hand and removed it from her face. "I really like movies."

"Okay." His manner was quietly encouraging.

"I wanted to see how they got made. Learn about things. Have some breathing space."

He nodded.

"I'm afraid you'll think I'm using you again."

He shook his head.

"It's just that... Remember what you said that first night we went out? When we walked on the beach after dinner? About always making up stories in your head, and thinking about why people do what they do, and wanting to get it down on paper and hoping it wouldn't be boring?"

He smiled.

She studied her jeans-clad knees as if they were vitally interesting. She couldn't meet his eyes.

"I can't think of anything more wonderful than writing for the movies."

The silence was deafening. She was just about ready to get up and leave, never see Joe again, when he took her hand. He held it gently, without any sort of sexual overtone, and it felt just right.

Perfect.

"Think you could help me salvage this thing?" he asked, indicating the script on the table in front of them.

"What?"

"I don't think Betsy is that well-rounded a character. And there are some other problems I can't quite figure out how to resolve yet."

Her heart picked up speed as she looked at him. Joe had actually had the courage to finish a script, and he was asking for her opinion. In Nina's eyes, it was nothing short of a miracle.

She'd never told him of that afternoon in Italy, about Jonathan's contempt for her thoughts, and everyone else's laughter at the idea of her rewriting a movie in her head. She'd only revealed that Brad had been involved with one of their friends.

Now Joe was actually *asking* her what she thought.

"The script was wonderful," she said, and her voice felt rusty. Her throat was sore from a particular kind of emotional disuse, but with each word, she felt herself growing stronger. "But there was this part in the beginning of act two..."

They sat close together on the pull-out couch, and neither noticed it was half-past three in the morning. The lights from the swimming pool in the large courtyard played over the ceiling of Joe's apartment as Nina began to tell him in detail what she thought of his script.

Looking back, she would always consider that night the beginning of their journey together.

HE STILL hadn't touched her, but it didn't bother her. They were close in other ways, she felt closer to him than anyone else in the world. Even Walter. For though she loved her friend deeply, she and Joe had a creative bond that grew stronger as the weeks passed.

She became a regular member of his acting class, and while she never became that good at improvisation and felt sick to her stomach every time she had to stand up and do a scene, Joe had been dead-on in his assessment of that class. There was nothing like actually being up on stage to see what worked and what didn't.

He talked her into a writing class at UCLA, through the university's extension program. And she found herself looking forward to their Wednesday-night forays into Westwood. And again, he made it clear to anyone who approached her that they were a team. A couple, in every sense of the word.

Brad sent a terse letter to her lawyer, refusing to sign the divorce papers until he'd talked to her personally. She didn't confide in Joe, ashamed at the way her plans for a divorce had deteriorated. She called her husband one morning from a pay phone in Beverly Hills, and realized his pride had been wounded more than anything else.

"You made me a laughingstock among all our friends, Nina, running away like that! How do you think that makes me look!"

She couldn't bring herself to care.

Work progressed on Joe's script, and when they felt it was as good as it could be, they started on another. Between the two of them, they had more self-discipline than either would have had alone. They worked long hours together, and the pile of pages slowly began to grow.

Joe's apartment became something of a salon. Friends they made through their various classes dropped in during the evening, and the conversations that flowed around Nina made her feel more alive than she'd felt in her entire life. There was just something about knowing you were on the right path, pushing yourself to the best of your abilities.

And Joe was the emotional center, endlessly helping, always teaching in his own forthright way. He had both male and female friends, but never gave her any cause to be jealous of the latter.

They had separate apartments, but practically lived with each other.

She had never known such happiness. But deep inside, she worried about her ex-husband. Even though they weren't divorced yet, she thought of him as an ex. Her instincts told her he wouldn't give up until he found her and confronted her.

It turned out she knew him even better than she thought.

THAT AFTERNOON, they'd taken a short break from their work on Joe's computer. She'd gone back to her apartment to fetch a particular book they needed for reference when she heard the brisk knock on the door. Thinking it was Joe, she opened it.

Brad stepped in, filling the doorway, pushing her back, slamming the door behind them.

She wanted to scream, but her throat closed and her entire body stilled.

His contempt for her apartment was obvious as he took in the crowded shelves piled with books, scripts and papers. His glance encompassed the single room, the bed against one wall, the few pieces of clothing piled at the foot of it, the grouping of plants she'd carefully arranged to catch what little sunlight made it beyond the shade of the huge banana tree at her window.

"You left me for *this*," he said, and his quiet rage was so much more frightening than outright anger would have been.

She didn't dare answer.

"You stupid little—"

"No." The minute she said the word, she knew she'd made a serious mistake. But she couldn't let him see it. "No, I'm not stupid."

He smiled then, but it didn't reach his beautiful blue eyes. "You're coming home with me, Nina. Your mother has been worried about you."

That much she knew was a lie.

She shook her head. "I want you to leave. Now."

"I want you to leave. Now." He mimicked her with cutting cruelty, then laughed softly.

"Get out before I call the police."

She started toward the phone, but he cut her off, grabbing her by the arm and twisting sharply, then pulling her after him until he had her pinned up against the far wall, his body pressed against hers.

"You thought you were pretty smart, didn't you?"

She struggled, determined to get away from him. But she was no match for his physical strength.

"Don't you want to know how I found you?"

She continued trying to break free, and his hold on her tightened.

"I hired a detective. He followed the money and spotted you at the bank one afternoon. Followed you right back here and watched you for several days before he phoned and let me know he'd found you."

She'd been watched. It gave her a sick feeling to know how deeply Brad had invaded her privacy.

"Let . . . go."

He laughed again, a quiet, utterly chilling sound, then adjusted his stance so his lips were against her ear.

"Who is he, Nina? The dark-haired guy? Did you run away with him? What did he give you that I didn't?"

He didn't want her. He'd never really wanted her. He was only enraged because he perceived another male had poached on his property.

She never knew what she might have said in return, for as she continued to struggle against Brad's hold, Joe walked into the room.

He assessed the situation in a heartbeat, and within seconds had Brad up against the wall in a chokehold. Nina fell to the floor, her legs didn't seem to want to work as she crawled toward the bed.

She'd never seen Brad truly frightened before, but now he was. His eyes bulged out of his head, his face flushed a dark red. He squirmed in Joe's grasp, much like a repulsive insect pinned to a display board.

"She's my...*wife,* damn you!" he managed to choke out.

"You gave up every right you had the first time you hit her."

She'd never seen Joe this angry. He'd told her about the fights he'd been in, but she'd never seen him in action, and she couldn't look away.

He simply pinned Brad against the wall, letting her husband's panic build as he told him what the new terms were.

"I'm going to let you go and you're going to leave. You're never coming back. And you're going to give Nina her freedom, because I'm going to marry her."

She blinked, not certain she'd heard him correctly. Her hands groped for the bed, and she pulled herself up on to it and sat down, still shaking. Joe had everything under control, but reaction had set in and she was helpless against her body's instinctive response.

Brad was terrified, but also humiliated with masculine rage. He'd been bested, and he knew it. Joe walked him out of the apartment. She heard them stumble down the stairs through the open apartment door, then the sound of Brad being thrown down the front, tiled stairs.

She'd slid off the bed and was sitting on the floor beside it, her back against the mattress, when Joe returned. He didn't talk, he simply took her in his arms and held her.

Walter came to the door, concern clear in his expression.

"What the hell happened?"

Joe told him, his voice calm, all the while holding her. Then he asked their friend and landlord if the one-bedroom apartment at the back of the building was still for rent.

"Sure."

"We're moving into it. I don't want her living alone."

By nightfall they'd moved in together. And until the divorce papers came through he never left her side.

He wanted to marry her, and she wasn't sure how she felt about that.

"Can't we just live together for a while?"

The look he gave her told her what he thought of that arrangement.

But he knew she was scared, so he let her be. They went back to work on their second script, and one afternoon, with papers spread out all over the living-room floor of their apartment, she looked up and found him watching her.

"I'm more trouble than I'm worth, aren't I?" she asked him suddenly, the words slipping out of her mouth before she could stop them.

He shook his head. He was sitting in the chair by the desk, making corrections on the computer while she checked the final copy for errors. Now she watched as he saved the material, turned the machine off and lay down on the floor next to her.

"You don't get it."

"What?"

"The French have an expression for it. *Coup de foudre.* The lightning bolt. It hits you when you see someone and you're never the same."

It took a moment for his meaning to sink in, then all she could do was stare.

"Me? The lightning bolt hit you when you first saw me?"

He nodded, watching her, waiting for her reaction.

She'd fought against loving him, not wanting to lose his friendship if something should go wrong. But now, lying on the rug with the man she loved and knowing he'd made himself so vulnerable, and knowing he *hated* being vulnerable, she knew she could no longer hold out against the emotional onslaught that was Joe Morrissey.

"It was the same for me," she whispered.

"What about the one-night stand?"

That still bothered him, and she didn't blame him. "It was just me, talking to myself and trying to muddle up something that was perfectly simple."

He slid over on the rug and took her into his arms. They were lying side by side, and he pressed his forehead against hers.

"Marry me?" he whispered.

"In a heartbeat," she said.

HE TOOK HER to meet all his relatives that same week.

She was nervous, but Joe's mother, Carmen, put her at ease immediately. A tiny woman, barely five feet tall, she had dark eyes and hair, and that certain ageless quality some Latin women possess.

She lived in a little house in Hollywood, surrounded by palms, banana trees and bamboo. Huge apartment buildings had been built up around her small house, and even though Carmen had been offered good money for her property, she kept it.

It was home.

She'd prepared quite a party for them, because Joe had told her they were getting married. A buffet table practically groaned under the weight of various highly spiced dishes. Black beans and rice, picadillo, and *ropa vieja*. One of Joe's aunts had married a man from Puerto Rico, so there was also a stew of chicken and rice, the *asopao,* and fried plantains. The centerpiece was a huge white cake in the midst of tropical flowers, garnished with toasted coconut and flavored with dark, spiced rum.

Colorful paper lanterns had been hung in the backyard, their lights brilliant against the night sky. It seemed to Nina that Joe had hundreds of relatives, aunts and uncles and cousins. But it was his mother who was the backbone of this particular family.

Where Nina had thought she might find a threatening matriarch, she discovered she and Carmen had something very basic in common. They both loved Joe.

The party continued late into the evening. One of Joe's uncles, a musician, played the guitar and managed a band. When the music began, drifting out over the cool night air, Joe came across the lawn to claim her.

It was charmingly old-fashioned, the way he led her out onto the large concrete patio that had been transformed into a dance floor for the occasion. All around them, friends and relatives applauded, and Nina knew she'd been accepted into the family.

She didn't know how to do these particular dances, so he taught her. That side of him that was so Latin was graceful and surefooted on a dance floor, and all that Nina knew was that she felt safe in his arms.

It was another form of lovemaking, dancing with Joe, and a perfectly acceptable means of expressing their love while his family watched, nodding their heads with approval.

He'd bought her an engagement ring, a tiny diamond she treasured far more than the ostentatious jewels that had been set in the rings she'd left behind in London. It winked in the lantern light as she rested her hand on Joe's shoulder, and Nina couldn't remember an evening she'd been happier.

They danced and celebrated into the night, and within the week, she found herself standing next to Joe and repeating vows that finally had some meaning for her.

They drove up the coast to Santa Barbara for their honeymoon, and spent the weekend at a tiny bed and breakfast.

And had their first major argument.

SEX HAD NEVER BEEN a cause for argument between them, for she had found a stunning, beautiful eroticism with Joe, and loved giving him pleasure.

But money soon was.

"It's a trust fund, Joe! I can do whatever I want with it, and I don't want you to go back to work! I want you to write full-time!"

"Your grandmother gave that money to *you*, Nina! I won't spend your money!"

Fighting with him, she saw both sides of his heritage, the blindly stubborn Irishman and the proud, Latin man who had to take care of his own. Who would rather die than let a woman support him.

He'd never realized just how wealthy she was.

The trust fund stood between them throughout most of their honeymoon, and she found it difficult to talk about it once they returned to Hollywood. Joe silently perused the want ads, determined to go back to work and write in his spare time. His funds had run out, and they had completed two screenplays during that time.

Nina decided she would take over the business end of their writing career. She called the writer's guild and sent in for their list of accredited agents, then began calling and sending their scripts out.

She had no idea the type of work Joe had decided on.

She knew her money made him uneasy, that he felt he was supporting her inadequately. Each time she tried to tell him she'd never been happier, it seemed she made the situation worse.

Brad might have hit her, but he'd easily been able to support her in the manner she was accustomed to. Now every time Joe looked at her, she knew he saw his own inadequacies reflected back at him. It was hopeless trying to tell her husband he'd given her far more than anyone else ever had.

He went out one evening on a job, and she found out what he was up to when he came back very late that same night. She hadn't slept at all, and as soon as she heard the key in the lock, she got out of bed and went to him.

He seemed tired, but he tossed a manila envelope on the coffee table, then went into the small kitchen and took a Coke out of the refrigerator.

"Check it out," he called to her. She reached for the envelope, and was astonished at the amount of cash it contained.

"Where did you get this?"

"I earned it."

She thought of his neighborhood, of the various ways boys and men made money, and rejected the notion instantly. Joe wouldn't do anything illegal. But if he hadn't, where had he gotten this kind of cash?

"Are you . . . are you okay?" she asked, wondering how to ask him what he was up to. He hadn't volunteered the information, and that in itself was significant.

"Yeah. I think I'm going to take a hot bath and go straight to bed."

He undressed in the bathroom, and through a crack in the barely open door, she saw the fresh, dark bruises on that beautiful body. And she knew.

"Joe," she said softly, at the bathroom door. "Can I come in?"

"Sure."

She went in. He was lying in the bathtub, stretched out, his head back against the tile. And he looked so utterly weary she felt her eyes fill.

"Joe," she said, kneeling down beside the tub and touching his cheek. "Joe." Her throat closed as she thought of all the things she wanted to tell him. She had to choose her words carefully, for he was a proud man, this husband of hers.

"You're fighting."

He looked at her for a long moment, then nodded.

"Boxing?"

"Yeah."

"How does it—how do you—"

"I win, I make money. I lose, I don't."

She thought of the world he'd grown up in, so different from her own. And though she knew he would never let her support him, she had to try.

"What if..." She swallowed against the sudden trembling in her throat. "What if we took another six months' worth of money out of the fund—"

"No, Nina—"

"We could see what happened with the scripts I sent out—"

"I can't take your money—"

"—then when something sold—"

He got up out of the tub, and she saw the full extent of his bruises. This hadn't been a carefully regulated fight like the kind you saw on television, or even in the movies. This had been a fight in a gym in one of the city's tougher neighborhoods, with local men putting in their money for a chance to watch two men bloody each other in battle.

"No," he said quietly, reaching for a towel. "There's six months' worth of expenses in that envelope if we live pretty tight. In two more fights, I'll have us covered for another six, with a little to spare. Then I'll sit down and write the screenplay that'll get us out of this dump."

He'd never thought of their apartment as a dump before. She thought of the hours they'd talked and laughed, painting and cleaning, rearranging furniture. They'd been so happy here, before the knowledge of her trust fund, but now their apartment was a dump.

"Joe." She followed him into their small bedroom as he toweled his hair dry. He'd cut it when he'd begun his job search, and now it barely brushed the back of his neck.

"Don't, Nina. The subject's closed."

But it couldn't be closed for her. "I don't want you giving up on every dream you ever had because you think I want—I want something better than this!"

"Better than this?" The expression in his eyes was mocking, self-deprecating. "What could be better than this?" His gesture encompassed the tiny bedroom, and even with a fresh coat of paint and the colorful curtains she'd put up, Nina saw it through his eyes for the first time.

"I thought it was for better or worse, Joe."

He silenced her with a look. When he finally spoke, it seemed as if the words were torn out of him.

"You could've done a whole lot better—"

"No!" She was at his side in an instant, her arms around his neck, holding on to him as if she couldn't bear to let go. "No. You don't understand. I didn't have anything until I met you." She lowered her voice to a whisper, tried to calm the sickening pounding of her heart. "I didn't even have myself."

"Nina, listen to me." He sat her down on their bed, then joined her.

"It's just the way it is. Two more fights, and we'll be out of the woods. And if we can't sell something in the next year, I'll fight some more."

"I know the kind of fighting you do. What if you get hurt... What if—"

He eased her down on the bed beside him and held her as she cried. But once Joe made up his mind about something, he couldn't be deterred from the path he'd chosen.

"Why are you doing this to us?" she finally whispered. The thought of anything happening to him was more than she could bear. The thought that she might be behind it was unendurable.

He didn't answer, and she closed her eyes. They lay in bed, side by side like spoons. She was quiet for such a long time she almost jumped when she felt his hand in her hair, stroking her head.

"I just . . . I want you to be proud of me."

He never would have said the words out loud, so she knew he thought she was asleep. And she felt sick and confused at the thought that her grandmother's money had brought so much confusion and unhappiness into their lives.

That she had brought him to this point in his life.

I just want you to be proud of me.

Tears slid silently down her cheeks.

Oh, Joe. I already am. . . .

Chapter Five

He didn't let her see any of his fights. She didn't even know about them until after the fact, when he gave her an envelope filled with money.

Until one night, when a phone call came after he left. With some tricky manipulating, Nina learned the location of that night's fight.

She grabbed her leather jacket and ran down the hall to Walter's front apartment, then told him of her plan.

"Do you know where you're talking about going?" he asked her, once she gave him the address. "That's one nasty neighborhood."

"I'm going whether you come with me or not."

"Nina—"

"Don't try to stop me."

He recognized blind stubbornness when he saw it, and after calling a friend of his so as to have safety in numbers, they were out the door and inside Nina's old Dodge.

Charlie, Walter's friend, was six feet five inches tall, muscular, bald and black. He had a pierced nose. No one would want to mess with him, which was exactly why Walter had requested his company. They picked him up on the corner of Fairfax and Fountain and continued downtown.

The three of them entered the run-down gym, and Nina, although she'd been pretty sure what she was going to find, found her heart aching for Joe.

The large room smelled, of sweat and smoke and despair. A huge crowd had gathered around the ring, their voices raised, shouting both encouragement and jeers.

Joe and his opponent were already facing off.

This was no regulated fight, with boxing gloves and headguards, mouthpieces and rules. Neither man even had his fists taped. This was a no-holds-barred, barefisted brawl, the winner determined by whoever was left standing at the end.

And though Nina had thought she'd seen violence, nothing in her life had prepared her for this fight.

She would have run straight to her husband if Walter hadn't grabbed her around the waist.

"Joe!" It was a cry from the deepest depths of her soul, torn out of her. The noise and excitement in the dirty, smoky room were so overwhelming he didn't hear her.

His opponent was a big, fleshy brute, with red hair and huge, meaty fists. Joe was quicker, moving around the ring, baiting, leading, then darting in for the quick kill. The crowd roared each time he scored a punch, and Nina screamed each time he took one.

He stayed on his feet, and it seemed to her he was fighting on sheer adrenaline, willing himself to keep going until his opponent got careless and gave him an opening.

He was fast, he was smart, he was passionate. He could fight, and the crowd absolutely loved him. Nina watched, as he even put a little flourish into what he did, fighting and entertaining the crowd at the same time. But never taking his eyes off his adversary.

The bell rang, and each man returned to his corner of the ring. Nina broke away from Walter's grasp, and began to push her way through the crowd. She'd caught the violence of the moment, the mob's frenzy, and nothing was going to stop her from reaching Joe's side.

She climbed up toward her husband, grasping the ropes before anyone there realized her intent. She got a quick glimpse of him before he saw her, and noticed the cut above his left eye, and an ugly purplish bruise beginning to blossom on his side.

When he saw her, he went perfectly still, but his dark eyes registered his fury.

"Joe, I—"

"Walter, get her out of here."

"Joe, please—"

"Get out! I can't fight with you here."

The bell rang, and she felt Walter's hand on her shoulder, then his arm was around her and he was guiding her back through the packed crowd, away from the ring, toward the main door and the cool, fresh night air outside.

All the way home she remembered how Joe had looked in the ring. She couldn't reconcile the gentle man she lived with, worked with, with the angry fighter she'd seen at that gym.

By the time he got home, she'd almost convinced herself she was terrified of him.

But when he walked in the door, he was simply her husband.

With a bandaged, broken nose. And another envelope full of money.

She simply stared at him, then turned around and walked into their bedroom. He followed her, and threw the envelope down on the bed.

"Don't you ever pull something like that again. Do you understand me?"

He hadn't wanted her to see that particular side of his life. She understood that now.

He was angry with her, so angry, but he'd never laid a hand on her and she was absolutely sure he wasn't going to start.

"No more, Joe."

He didn't answer, simply stared at her for a long moment, then looked away and started to unbutton his shirt.

The sight of his chest made her come apart.

He was bruised. She'd seen the size of his opponent, and knew it had taken everthing Joe possessed to win tonight's match She didn't even remember taking that first step, but then she was in his arms and he was holding on to her, staggering a bit.

She realized he was exhausted, and eased him down on the bed. Without a word, she undressed him and helped him beneath the covers. He closed his eyes as sleep claimed him, and within minutes was breathing deeply.

She sat on the bed next to him and wondered if it was truly over. Now that she'd seen, now that she knew what went on, she couldn't bear to see him walk out that door, knowing where he was going.

It might not be the same, seedy, run-down gym, but it would be the same sort of fight. And one night he might not be so lucky.

Joe moved in his sleep, muttering something, and the envelope he'd thrown on the bed fell to the floor. It opened, and a thick wad of bills fell out. She gathered them up, counting them as she did so, and realized tonight's fight had brought in almost double the money the first one had.

He must have been taking a greater risk.

She put the money carefully away in their top dresser drawer, then lay down beside her sleeping husband and wondered how she could ensure he'd never have to fight again.

SHE WOKE UP later that night, feeling the mattress depress gently, then realizing Joe was getting out of their bed. Nina lay silently until she heard him go into the bathroom. The shower came on, and she knew he had to be hurting, both physically and emotionally.

She wondered at these walls they built, two intelligent people who loved each other so very deeply. And she knew he was proud, and was fighting for a peculiarly masculine feeling, ensuring he felt like a man. Her money somehow diminished him in his own eyes, and there was nothing she could do about it.

But there were other ways they could communicate, and certainly without fighting. She and Joe had never had trouble in bed, except for the fact that she still felt frozen inside and couldn't give over that final part of herself to her husband.

It was nothing he did, she'd assured him of that over and over. He'd questioned her at first, gently, assuring her he would do anything she wanted or needed. She'd been emotionally devastated, remembering the worst of her first marriage.

Perhaps Brad had been right in his assessment of her. Perhaps she was cold. But her intuition told her that her ex-husband's opinion of her was utterly false. She couldn't be cold, not when she burned when she wrote, when she worked. And she burned with the strongest of emotions when she was with Joe, when he touched her, looked at her, made love to her.

She just couldn't seem to trust herself to let go.

And she couldn't quite explain it to him. She simply asked for time, and he stopped giving that particular problem a voice. But she knew he was aware of what happened—or didn't happen—every time they made love.

She understood he wanted to make her his own, but it wasn't in a way that diminished her. It didn't make her less than what she was. She sat up in bed as it suddenly connected in her mind, how helpless and vulnerable Joe had to feel.

In his own eyes, he couldn't support her in the fashion she was accustomed to. He couldn't fully satisfy her in their bed. He had to be looking at their marriage and considering his end of the contribution a complete failure.

How ironic. He'd given her so much, yet considered himself a failure.

And no wonder he fought. The type of boxing Joe did not only paid the bills and salvaged his pride, it allowed him to give expression to the anger and frustration that had to be eating away at his insides.

The shower was still running as she slipped out of her nightgown and walked toward the darkened bathroom.

He looked up when she opened the stall door. He'd been leaning against the tile, letting the hot water beat down on his sore and bruised muscles. Now, even in the dim outside lighting from the small bathroom window, she could see his eyes narrow and could sense his reluctance to have her there.

She ignored the feelings she felt from him and stepped into the stall, closing the door behind her. Hot, wet steam assaulted her as she picked up a bar of soap and began to wash his back.

He didn't relax for quite a while, but she finally felt the tension in his body ease as she kept touching him.

She tried to offer comfort with her touch. Words were so inadequate. Words got them into trouble every time. For two people who considered themselves writers, with words their stock-in-trade, it was a humbling realization that sometimes the most perilous of emotions couldn't be put into that finite a form of expression.

She washed him as tenderly as a mother might a child, but offered comfort as a lover. His face seemed alien, with the white bandage across his nose so startling against his tanned face. Only his eyes, ever-watchful, waiting for another argument to begin, told her she was still with Joe and everything had to be all right.

She would make it all right.

She had put the soap back and was rinsing her hands off when he moved, pinning her up against the tiled surface of the shower stall. She felt his body against hers, and knew he was no longer relaxed, but looking for another kind of comfort. She knew why, and knew she would give it to him.

His face was shadowed as she looked up at him, but she could still see various emotions flit across his features, feelings she knew he was keeping tightly in check. She didn't want to talk, and she ran her fingers through his thick, dark hair, pulling it gently. Pulling it until he lowered his mouth and took hers, kissed her, filled her with a sweetness that stole her breath away.

She was ready for him in an instant, as wanting him had never been a problem. He left the water running as he picked her up and carried her to their bed. He laid her down among the rumpled sheets, both of them still wet from the shower, then covered her with his body. He touched her, testing her readiness, then entered her with a strong, sure thrust, joining their bodies with an emotional desperation that wasn't lost on her.

He made love to her with such feeling, kissing her as he stroked her, murmuring words of love and encouragement, touching her. Keeping himself firmly in check. Then moving away from her, kissing his way down her body, taking her in that other way that made her cry out and grab his head in her hands.

And a part of her wondered what she was doing to him, denying him that part of her pleasure. What she was doing to herself—and to them.

They both had their fears about making this marriage work, but she could certainly do away with a few of hers. Especially one so crucial to their joining together.

He slid up her body, then took her into his arms and urged her against him. His lips found her breasts, his fingers cupped her, found her, stroked her until her legs trembled and fell apart, until she began that beautiful process of feminine surrender.

He watched her as he touched her, lying next to her. Before she would have shut her eyes or turned her face away. There was still something about him that frightened her, a repressed violence she'd seen tonight. She thought of the way he'd lashed out with his fists with such pure masculine rage, and thought of those same fingers touching her so intimately.

She couldn't look away from him, it was as if she were discovering him all over again. He touched her with a stronger pressure and she moved into the intimate caress. Then she bit down on trembling lips to still a cry barely forming, still waiting for release.

"Don't," he whispered, his voice rough and low. Emotional. She was touching him in a different way, but just as deeply.

He moved so his lips were against her ear, and still touched her, stroked her, aroused her.

"Scream the place down if you want to," he said.

She took a deep breath, and was shocked at the sound that came out of her mouth. Anguished. Alive.

"That's it, baby. That's good."

Everything centered on what Joe was doing to her, on her own body, hot and wet and burning. She urged him on top of her and he slid between her thighs and took her again. Her head fell back, one hand reached out and grabbed at the headboard of their brass bed. Her fingers tightened reflexively around the cool metal as her body responded to his.

Taking his weight on his forearms, Joe assaulted her senses, pushing inside her with a slow, steady rhythm. For an instant, she was ashamed of the noise they were making, springs squeaking, the sounds rising out of the back of her throat. She'd never given voice to them before, but now it was as if she couldn't stop them.

She'd always shut down at a certain point, allowing herself to go so far and no farther. Now she felt him opening her farther, pushing her legs up and apart, pushing deeper, stroking, touching, burning, feeling—

"Give it to me, Nina," he whispered against her ear. "Give me what I want."

And it happened. So suddenly, so swiftly, and so completely. She lost herself in it, couldn't tell where she began and he ended, clung to him as she opened farther, became more vulnerable, bloomed erotically.

Coup de foudre, he'd said. This was another lightning bolt, and it shook her to her soul.

AFTERWARD, she curled herself against him, exhausted. And wondered why she'd found it so very hard to give over to him. To herself. To anyone.

He spoke to her softly, and what he said shocked her.

"I won't fight anymore—if you don't want me to."

She'd thought she'd felt everything a woman could feel tonight, and the rush of tears surprised her. Burying her face in his shoulder, she held on to him tightly.

"Please," she whispered against his neck. "I couldn't—I didn't—"

"Shh." He rubbed her back, held her until she stopped crying, then grabbed a few tissues from the nightstand so she could blow her nose. She was sitting up in bed when he tickled her foot.

She laughed, then slid down into bed with him. The sheets were still damp, but it was a hot night and they felt cool, not uncomfortable, against her skin.

He kissed her forehead, then stroked it with the pad of his thumb.

"This," he whispered, "baffles me."

She turned on her side so she could see his face. She cupped his cheek with one hand, then kissed him.

"The feeling's mutual. I never know what you're thinking."

He laughed then, and she smiled, sensing the worst was over. He wasn't going to fight anymore. He'd promised her, and she'd never known Joe to break a promise.

"This," he said, tracing one nipple with his index finger, "fascinates me."

She felt her face heating as her body responded, the nipple hardening until the tip of her breast felt unbearably sensitive to his touch.

She covered his hand with her own, wanting to stop the sensation. He did, but kept his hand on hers. Then slowly, sliding it over his hot, hair-roughened body, he closed it over his erection.

"Again?" she whispered.

"I didn't..."

"Oh...*oh!*" She slid farther beneath the covers, letting go of him, wondering how she could have possibly been more selfish than she'd been tonight. Taking so much, and giving so little.

"It didn't bother me. I liked it a lot."

She touched him again, stroking softly, arousing him. She kissed him, darting her tongue into his mouth and feeling him grow even harder in her hand.

"I don't know why—"

"Shh, baby, you don't have to explain."

"I want to."

"And I want to make it good for you."

She looked at him, loving what she saw. His eyes were bright and hot and alive. He could give her this, what they found together in bed.

Men were funny. He had no idea how much he'd already given her, before tonight. She doubted she'd ever be able to make him understand.

He baffled her, but she loved him. Wanted him.

The feeling was obviously mutual.

They didn't leave their bedroom for two days, and when they did, it was to begin working together all over again.

SHE WAS HAPPIER than she'd ever been, and she knew Joe was, too. Now, with everything going so well, it was time to put yet another phase of their plan into action.

Only this was a phase she wanted to surprise him with.

Nina signed up for a class at UCLA on public relations, agents and the business of writing and selling a screenplay. But what she was really interested in was the third of the eight classes, when six agents came to talk about representation.

They hadn't had a whole lot of luck mailing their screenplays out. Either no one was reading, and they were rebuffed early on over the phone, or they received the scripts back with a standard rejection letter.

Now, Nina decided to catch the lion in his own den.

She drove down to Beverly Hills and took a considerable amount of money out of her trust fund. Then she went to Rodeo Drive and shopped until she found the most beautiful business suit she could find. Stunning shoes. A gorgeous blouse.

One thing her mother had given her was a knowledge of clothing, an appreciation of quality no matter what the price. She knew what she looked good in, and she knew if she and Joe were to get ahead, she had to shed her faded jeans and enter the world of business.

Like Joe's phoenix, she had to transform herself.

Then she went to one of the better salons and had her hair cut and styled, highlighted and blown dry. She wasn't as clever with her hair, and asked the stylist numerous questions as to how to achieve the same effects at home.

Makeup was the last stop, and a knowledgeable and delighted saleswoman helped her pick out flattering shades among the newest colors.

Once everything was at home and in her closet, it was only a matter of time.

SHE RESEARCHED each agent expected at the class, and decided she liked Arnie Axel the best.

He'd been around a long time. His father and grandfather had both worked in the studios, and had known many of the greats. Arnie had found out early on, according to what she read about him at the Hollywood library, that he liked working with actors and writers. He liked channeling their creativity into prosperous and successful careers.

She and Joe worked furiously on their third script. She told him about the class, but not what she planned to do afterward. What she planned would be an effort for her, for despite the coolness some people sensed in her, she was desperately shy underneath. But she would do anything for Joe.

The agents were charming, and interspersed facts with interesting stories. Nina sat in the front row and studied Arnie Axel.

She liked him. A lot. Gray-haired and chubby, he reminded her of an overgrown elf. But he had a shrewd sense of the market, and he clearly respected creativity.

When the evening came to an end, she wasted no time.

"Mr. Axel?"

He was putting some papers in a briefcase, and looked up with a guarded smile.

"Could I buy you a drink? I enjoyed your talk tremendously."

He assessed her within seconds, and she knew she might look the part of another Beverly Hills trophy wife who filled her evenings by taking classes and playing at various careers. She held her breath, waiting.

He must have seen something he liked.

"Certainly."

His car was waiting outside, and they went to a nearby restaurant in Westwood. Once their drinks were in front of them, Arnie leaned forward.

"You're looking for representation?" His tone was still guarded, and Nina couldn't blame him.

"Yes, I am. My partner and I." She swallowed.

"We've finished two screenplays, and we're almost done with a third."

Now she sensed an interest.

"Do you have them with you?"

She nodded her head. She'd brought a briefcase of her own. It was highly unorthodox, what she was doing, but she'd tried the conventional route and it was taking both her and Joe nowhere fast.

As she laid the two scripts on the table in front of them, she said quickly, "Joe wrote the first one, I made a few suggestions he incorporated. The second was more a true collaboration, and the third is, as well."

"So you've been representing him?"

"In a way." She quickly told him what they'd done thus far, and all the rejection they'd encountered. Then she mentioned a few of the things she'd learned about the agent's career, and how she'd picked him out of tonight's lineup.

Arnie paused for a long moment, and Nina wondered if she'd gone too far.

"I'm very flattered."

"What clinched it for me was what you said tonight about always taking the time to read new people. And I wanted to have just a moment to talk with you, away from the others. I thought—if you had a face to associate with the script, we might have a better chance."

He tapped the script lightly with one of his pudgy fingers.

"A good screenplay is solid gold. You know that, don't you? But it has to be here. If it's not on the page, I can't sell it."

She took a deep breath, remembering their endless rewrites.

"It's as good as we can make it. But if you want rewrites, we're willing to do that, too."

She didn't overstay her welcome once the scripts were in his hands, merely paid their tab, thanked him and headed back toward her car.

At home, she told Joe what had happened, and for the first time in their married life she stunned her husband into silence.

"Arnie Axel? *The* Arnie Axel? You had a *drink* with him?"

"The one and only." His reaction was everything she'd hoped for, and she found she liked surprising him.

Baffling him.

He'd taken in the new suit and shoes, her hair and makeup. Even her perfume. Now a certain masculine recognition dawned in his eyes, and Nina held up her hand to forestall the inevitable.

"Joe, no! Don't even say it."

"You have no idea the way men think."

"Oh, for God's sake, he's in his sixties if he's a day."

"And I'm sure he didn't find you at all attractive, dressed like that."

"I didn't do anything to give him the impression that—"

"Doesn't matter. Men are men."

"Men are men," she mimicked, throwing her purse down on the bed and starting to take the pins out of her hair. She pulled a brush through the thick, shoulder-length strands, then slung her jacket over the back of a chair.

"Is he married?"

"Divorced."

"Hah!"

"He has a girlfriend, Joe. I saw their picture in the *Times.*"

"And how old is she?" He'd come into the bedroom and was watching her undress.

She hesitated too long before answering, then said quickly, "In her thirties, I think."

"Great! A dirty old man, to boot!"

She shook her head, then unzipped her skirt and stepped out of it. The suit hadn't been the only thing she'd bought. Joe had deserved something, as well, and she'd stopped at the lingerie department and bought some of the sexiest underwear she'd ever indulged in.

Including a black lace garter belt and stockings.

Now, she deliberately unbuttoned her blouse, tossed it over the same chair, then shimmied out of her half-slip and picked up her hairbrush. Standing by her small vanity table, she continued brushing her hair, raising her arms and studying the effect in the mirror.

Twice that night, Joe was stunned into silence.

But not for long.

He came up behind her and took the brush out of her hand.

"What's this all about?" he whispered, his hand resting on the curve of her hip.

"Well, Arnie got to enjoy the suit, so I thought you deserved a little something, too."

He laughed, then turned her toward him. Hooking a finger into the top of the garter belt, against her stomach, he led her toward the bed.

"You're truly one of a kind, Nina."

His words elicited such pleasure, but soon after, she was feeling a different sort of pleasure, everything he was capable of giving her. And as far as she was concerned, the earth moved and the stars fell right out of the sky.

ARNIE LIKED both of them. He also liked their work, which was even better. The only thing was, there was no real market for their kind of script.

"What would you suggest we do?" Joe asked that afternoon in the agent's Beverly Hills office.

"There's one hot ticket in town right now. Robert Corbin is looking to change directions with his career."

"*The* Robert Corbin?" Nina asked.

Arnie nodded. "Corbin the Scorpion, as he's called in this town. He causes a lot of trouble on the set, but he can still open a film like no one else." He leaned back in his chair and reached for his coffee. "Thus, when Robert talks, Hollywood listens."

"What direction does he want to go in now?" Joe asked.

"Action-adventure. Look how well it's paid off for Willis, Seagal and Schwarzenegger. And these films make money overseas, because translating's a snap. Anyone in any language can understand an exploding car." He took a sip of his coffee. "Original ideas are great, but so are original turns on old ideas that have worked before."

"If we wrote something," Nina began cautiously, "could you get it to Corbin's people?"

"If you write something and it's all on the page, I can guarantee his people will not only look at it, they'll want to purchase it for him."

Joe stood up then, his own cup of coffee barely touched. "Then what are we doing here?" He grinned at Arnie. "The coffee's great, and so is the company, but Nina and I have a screenplay to write."

WITHIN A FEW WEEKS, John Blackheart was born. By the time they both got down to writing, they knew him as well as they knew themselves.

The script took form, and Nina could feel Joe's excitement. It almost hurt to hope, but she had a feeling this was the script that was at least going to get them looked at. It was too much to expect Corbin's representatives would actually buy it, but it might put them on the map.

Then they'd be on their way.

Six weeks later, they delivered a complete script to Arnie. He read it overnight, and suggested a few excellent changes. They made them within days, then resubmitted.

Arnie talked to Robert Corbin's people at an industry party. They expressed interest in the script. Several of his people read it, and passed it along to the star.

Then Robert Corbin gave them the single biggest break of their career. He liked their script, liked it enough to make an offer. And had enough star power to actually get it into production.

They went to see the film the day it opened, and sat toward the back. Holding Joe's hand, Nina felt as if she were breathing with the audience.

She knew the entire screenplay by heart. Robert Corbin had known excellent work when he read it and hadn't changed a thing, which was almost unheard of in the industry. But he'd trusted their vision, and given them the gift of seeing their work up on screen completely intact.

By the time the movie was half over, she was ecstatic. By the end of the movie she knew the audience didn't just like John Blackheart, they loved him. Men wanted to be like him and women wanted to be loved by him—as well as hit those satin sheets with him. She and Joe stayed in their seats while the credits rolled and listened to the audience response.

Word-of-mouth was incredible.

Deadly Threat blew away the competition that weekend, and went on to become the top grossing film that summer.

They'd created a hit, made it to that special, exalted place every writer dreams about. Straight to the moon and beyond to the stars. Delirious with happiness, they both spent the summer in a daze of perpetual bliss.

And neither of them even suspected it was the beginning of the end.

Chapter Six

Joe woke up early the next morning at Robert Corbin's compound and wondered exactly how he was going to win Nina back.

She was a handful.

I'm more trouble than I'm worth. She'd said so herself, that afternoon in their apartment, long ago when she'd finally agreed to marry him.

But life, and love, didn't always play fair. He'd been so furious after she'd left him, he'd gone on a masculine rampage of partying. He'd made it a point to meet most of L.A.'s female population. He'd even gone so far as to date several of them.

But none of them got to him the way Nina did. When that lightning bolt hit, it hit, and there was nothing he could do about it.

She was still angry with him, and he couldn't figure it out. Hadn't he done everything in his power to take care of her, to ensure her safety and happiness? Yes, they'd gotten too embroiled in the whole Hollywood game, but he'd wanted to be a success in her eyes. He'd wanted her to be proud of him.

She'd hit the roof if she realized he'd never actually signed the divorce papers. He'd simply slipped them in an envelope and mailed them back to her. Hurt and angry, he'd decided he wasn't going to let her go. Not yet.

She'd obviously stuck the return envelope in a drawer somewhere—typical Nina—or he would have heard from her, demanding to know why their divorce wasn't final.

So, they were still married in the eyes of the law.

And about as far apart emotionally as two people could be.

What to do?

Joe was nothing if not a long-range planner. It was a skill that had stood him in good stead while negotiating his way through the Hollywood jungle. Now he set his mind to work, plotting and planning.

The one thing they had in common, the one thing he knew they both loved with an emotional, unreasonable amount of passion, was the character of John Blackheart.

He could appeal to the writer in her. He could tell her they simply couldn't make that horrible last movie Blackheart's swan song. Even if they practically killed each other while writing the next Blackheart screenplay, they'd be moving closer in a strange kind of way.

At least they'd be feeling something. Anything was better than this emotional deadness, this emptiness and disillusionment.

Don't offer any resistance. Be the complete, compassionate, hardworking professional. That'll impress her.

He stared at the ceiling for several minutes, wondering if this entire approach was wise. Then he got up and headed for the shower.

He'd have to face Nina sooner or later, and there was no time like the present.

SHE WAS in the kitchen eating breakfast when Joe walked in.

She couldn't read him. Try as she might, she had no idea what he was going to do. She'd sat up most of the night remembering, wondering, working herself into an emotional state. Now, in the sunny, light-filled kitchen, eating Sam's wonderful banana-nut waffles, she kept her attention on the food in front of her.

It wasn't as if they couldn't actually leave if they really wanted to. Yes, alarms would go off, bells would ring, and everyone in the place would have been woken out of a sound sleep. She'd thought about leaving in the morning, after everyone was up. Just simply announcing she'd had enough, wanted out, and driving back to Los Angeles.

She didn't need the money; she still had her trust, enough money in it to last her the rest of her life and then some, if she invested wisely. It wasn't money that held her here.

It was Joe.

She considered herself a loser at marriage, two times up at bat, two times struck out. The second divorce had been far worse than the first, because she'd left Brad a long time before their separation became legal.

With Joe, she suspected she'd never quite make that necessary emotional break.

She'd felt so bad about leaving Joe, she'd done the divorce herself, out of one of those self-help law books. When the papers had arrived in the mail after he'd signed them, she'd felt so miserable and alone she'd simply crammed the envelope into her overflowing file cabinet.

It was there somewhere—she didn't really want to know where.

They were simply too close, that was the problem. Their lives were entwined too tightly. Friends, writers, lovers, spouses. It was a tangled web, and one she still hadn't learned how to emotionally negotiate.

He sat down across from her. She didn't look at him, feigning an inordinate amount of interest in her food. Sam approached the glass-topped table and set

"I think we should give it a try."

"You do?" She almost choked on her orange juice.

"Yeah, I do." He took a deep breath, then let it out slowly. "I can't let John retire with such a horrible last story."

Warmth flooded her. This, at least, she understood. Their marriage may not have worked, but they'd been extraordinarily blessed as writing partners.

She nodded her head. "I know."

"So, why don't we take the next forty-eight hours and see how it goes?"

"All right. I agree." She thought of spending the next two days in Joe's constant company, and knew she needed to restock her feminine arsenal. "But could I have this morning for a few errands? There's someone I promised to see."

His eyes narrowed as he focused on her, and for a moment Nina thought he was going to offer a protest. Then he nodded.

"Two o'clock, by the outdoor pool?"

"I'll bring my notes."

THE SOMEONE she'd promised to see was her old friend Diane, who operated an elegant salon on El Paseo. She'd called her the night before and begged for an emergency appointment, explaining the entire mess.

Now, in a chair, getting her blond hair streaked, Nina came clean with the entire story.

"You still love him? Tell him!" Diane was tall, with generous curves and bright red hair. Her makeup was dramatic, and she had the sort of open, uncomplicated personality that drew people to her in droves.

"Oh Di, I can't. What if he doesn't feel the same way?"

"Then what exactly were you planning on doing?"

Nina gave her friend a look.

"Well, I thought that as we worked together, we might form a tentative bond. Then, in the weeks ahead, we might end up—"

"In bed."

"The thought had crossed my mind."

"Nina, that's using him!"

"Somehow, I don't think Joe would look at it that way."

Diane sighed as she checked Nina's hair. "Go on."

"We were always good in bed."

"Yeah, you and any other woman he chose to sleep with."

Nina simply stared at the mirror, at her friend.

"Come on, Nina. Joe's got it, whatever it is. He's like catnip to women."

"He's probably been messing around, having all these wild affairs—"

PLAY
HARLEQUIN'S
LUCKY HEARTS
GAME

AND YOU COULD GET

- ★ **FREE BOOKS**
- ★ **A FREE CRYSTAL PENDANT NECKLACE**
- ★ **AND MUCH MORE**

→

TURN THE PAGE AND DEAL YOURSELF IN

PLAY "LUCKY HEARTS" AND YOU COULD GET...

★ Exciting Harlequin American Romance® novels—FREE

★ Plus a crystal pendant necklace—FREE

THEN CONTINUE YOUR LUCKY STREAK WITH A SWEETHEART OF A DEAL

1. Play Lucky Hearts as instructed on the opposite page.

2. Send back this card and you'll receive brand-new Harlequin American Romance® novels. These books have a cover price of $3.50 each, but they are yours to keep absolutely free.

3. There's no catch. You're under no obligation to buy anything. We charge nothing—ZERO—for your first shipment. And you don't have to make any minimum number of purchases—not even one!

4. The fact is thousands of readers enjoy receiving books by mail from the Harlequin Reader Service. They like the convenience of home delivery...they like getting the best new novels months before they're available in stores...and they love our discount prices!

5. We hope that after receiving your free books you'll want to remain a subscriber. But the choice is yours—to continue or cancel, anytime at all! So why not take us up on our invitation, with no risk of any kind. You'll be glad you did!

You'll look like a million dollars
when you wear this lovely necklace!
Its cobra-link chain is a generous
18" long, and the multi-faceted Austrian
crystal sparkles like a diamond!

DETACH AND MAIL CARD TODAY

THE HARLEQUIN READER SERVICE® : HERE'S HOW IT WORKS

Accepting free books places you under no obligation to buy anything. You may keep the books and gift and return the shipping statement marked "cancel." If you do not cancel, about a month later we will send you 4 additional novels, and bill you just $2.71 each plus 25¢ delivery and applicable sales tax, if any.* That's the complete price—and compared to cover prices of $3.50 each—quite a bargain! You may cancel at any time, but if you choose to continue, every month we'll send you 4 more books, which you may either purchase at the discount price ... or return at our expense and cancel your subscription.

*Terms and prices subject to change without notice. Sales tax applicable in N.Y.

BUSINESS REPLY MAIL
FIRST CLASS MAIL   PERMIT NO. 717   BUFFALO, NY

POSTAGE WILL BE PAID BY ADDRESSEE

HARLEQUIN READER SERVICE
3010 WALDEN AVE
PO BOX 1867
BUFFALO NY 14240-9952

NO POSTAGE
NECESSARY
IF MAILED
IN THE
UNITED STATES

"Oh, I don't know. There was this study done in which they found out men remarry quicker than women. They need us more than we need them."

"I can't believe that of Joe."

"He's only human, Nina. He's probably as nervous as you are."

She considered this as her friend finished her hair, then moved on to a facial, manicure and pedicure. She was just finishing her left hand with a delicate pink shade when Nina voiced the thought that had been troubling her all night.

"How could something so right have gone so wrong?"

"Aries and Taurus."

"What?"

"Aries and Taurus. Incendiary, inflammatory, incredible sex, but you've got to really work to get along. I did your relationship number, didn't I? Wasn't it a two? Opposites attract, but you've got to agree to disagree."

"What else?" Nina loved her friend's interest in astrology and numerology, and at this point she was willing to try anything.

"Let me think. Number two. You have to be sensitive to each other's needs, and give each other time alone. You click with Joe, but each of you needs time away in order to kind of regroup. Regain your strength."

"It makes sense. We used to be exhausted after we worked with each other."

"See?"

"So how do you think I should approach this?"

"Aries men are so proud. They can't bear to be laughed at. I think you may have to make the first move."

"What if he—"

"He won't. Look at it this way. Maybe the two of you just need to really go at it in order to see what it is you've lost. You haven't been to bed with anyone else, have you?"

She shook her head.

"I bet he hasn't, either."

"Oh, come on! We're talking eighteen months of celibacy. And Joe was—"

"A sex-crazed animal. But with you, Nina, not with anyone else. Did he ever cheat on you?"

"With what? We made love almost every night."

Diane smiled. "That's an Aries. Don't ask him to give up his sex life. Unless his heart is broken."

"You think—"

"I know. I never told you this, 'cause I didn't want to upset you. I saw Joe at a party in L.A., and he looked great. He could have taken home any of the women there, but he left alone."

"He probably met someone afterward."

"Play fair, Nina. Don't get that Taurean stubbornness up. I think he still isn't over you."

"When was this?"

"About three weeks ago."

She considered this as she paid her bill, then had a quick lunch with her friend. Afterward, Diane pointed her in the direction of another store.

"You're working by the pool this afternoon? There's a darling boutique three doors down, her bikinis are to die for. Get a few and see what happens."

"I thought you said I'd have to make the first move."

Her friend grinned. "You are. Think of it as setting the stage. My money's on Joe. Aries men are so wonderfully direct, I don't think he's going to disappoint you."

HE DIDN'T.

She sauntered out to the pool with the confidence born of knowing today, thanks to Diane, was a spectacular hair day. The facial had done the job, as well as a new and very natural-looking shade of blush. She'd even bought an ankle bracelet, and the tiny bell jingled as she walked over to the chaise lounge where Joe was stretched out.

SHE LOOKED incredible.

He couldn't stop staring at her until he finally forced himself to look away.

Her hair was different, and knowing she'd spent the morning in a salon relieved him. He'd thought she might have been meeting someone else, someone male, and the thought of that sort of encounter had been agonizing. If he'd known she was meeting someone of the opposite sex, he would have had serious thoughts about locking her away with him here at the compound and throwing away the key.

Her turquoise bikini was a lethal weapon in its own right. The only other jewelry she wore besides that ankle bracelet were gold hoops in her ears.

She was beautiful. But there was something about her that unnerved him. She was thinner, seemed paler, and he wondered if she had been missing him as much as he missed her.

There was only one way to find out.

"Okay, let's get to work."

HE LOOKED incredible.

His swimsuit was black and brief, the only other thing he wore was a gold cross around his neck. His mother had given it to him, and she'd never seen him take it off.

His body was darkly tanned, muscular, alive. So vital. Joe had a life force that had grabbed her from the start; she'd been attracted to the way he met the world head-on and forced it to come to terms with how he wanted things to be. His Hawaiian shirt was draped over the back of the chaise, along with the shorts he'd worn at breakfast.

Clyde completed the picture, stretched out beneath his master's lounge chair in a small bit of shade.

The January weather was absolutely perfect, warm with a hint of a breeze. The pool area had a view of mountains, desert and palm trees, and Nina sat down on the chaise next to Joe's and stretched out in the sun.

The sound of a pleased meow had her turning her head.

"Henry?"

The fat white cat came running up, his belly shaking. He leaped to the foot of her chaise, gave her toes a quick lick, then stretched out and basked his considerable bulk in the bright sunlight.

Joe was smiling when she glanced at him.

"He's quite a character, that guy."

Henry gave him a look, sighed, then rested his head on his paws and proceeded to take a nap.

"Okay," Joe said, legal pad in hand. "Do you have any notes?"

She'd been covertly studying him, and remembering. And wondering how long it was going to take before they found themselves in bed.

"What? Notes. Oh. Yeah, here they are. I came up with a few ideas yesterday, but none of them were that good."

"I know what you mean. You know, we could go into town this evening and rent the entire series. That might get us thinking again."

"That's a good idea. Where are your notes..."

IT WAS ALL he could do to look and not touch.

She'd been his wife once, in every sense of the word. And theirs had been a relationship filled with every pleasure that could transpire between a man and a woman. There had been no boundaries, Nina had been an adventurous, passionate and experimental lover, and he'd wanted her in the worst possible way.

Now, sitting less than three feet away from her, seeing her scantily clad body reclining on a chaise right next to him, was torture of the purest form. If he'd had his way, he would have joined her on that chaise, hooked his fingers in her bikini bottom, dragged it off and taken her right here by the pool.

She looked beautiful. Far better than she had the other night. Nina had that same cool beauty that Grace Kelly had possessed, that ice-princess persona that tempted a man to take her back to his bed and thaw her out. Joe knew from experience that her coolness masked a passion that burned as bright and hot as any woman's.

She had the heart of a rebel, and that had turned him on as much as her high-society looks had.

Her hair caught the light, sunlight sparking it with pure golden highlights. Her slender body was an expression of pure grace as she reclined on the lounger. The words that came to mind to describe her were *refined, cool* and *elegant*. But it was her eyes, with their cool, deep green shading that he'd loved to lose himself in, which brought back so many erotic, specific memories.

Nina, her head thrown back, her delicate throat arched, moving restlessly beneath him and giving him more pleasure than any woman before or since....

Nina, her head thrown back as she laughed and laughed as he tickled her on the couch.

And best of all, that satisfied smile he'd put on her face each night, and all the nights he'd watched her as she drifted off to sleep. Nina had been a conquest he'd had to make. Warming up that cool fire that was so much a part of her nature had been a challenge he hadn't been able to ignore.

He'd wanted her and he'd captured her. And he'd made a gigantic mess of the whole thing. But now she was his, for as long as it took them to finish this treatment. And before that time was up, he'd get her in bed. He'd make her his again in the most primitive way possible, and never let her go....

He realized she was talking to him and made a conscious, disciplined attempt to surface from this peculiar sensual haze.

"But if he's still divorced, like in the last film, then we could—"

Divorced? Who was she talking about? Blackheart. He came back to the present moment with a start.

"That was a mistake, getting divorced."

She stared at him for a heartbeat longer than normal, and he collected himself.

"Blackheart. It was a mistake, having him divorce his wife and bringing in that younger woman. One of the reasons people liked him was that he was a stable, married guy."

He watched as she wet her lips, then wrote something down on the spiral pad.

"He did love her, you know." He knew he was getting into deep water sooner than he would have liked, but Joe couldn't stop the words from coming out of his mouth.

"I know."

"He never understood why she left him."

He saw the warning signs in her eyes, but couldn't seem to stop.

"What was her motivation?" Nina asked, her tone very quiet and controlled.

"The writers never made that very clear. What do you think?"

She stood up. "I think I need to go for a short swim. Just to clear my head a bit."

He watched her as she walked to the shallow end of the large pool and stepped down into the cool, blue water. And he wondered. It wasn't like Nina to be so cautious. Normally she would have taken a dive off the board. It wasn't like her, to walk down those pool steps.

What the hell was going on?

SHE WAS out of her depth and she knew it.

How had she ever thought it was possible for the two of them to work together without first clearing up all the emotional baggage that tagged along after them?

He still wanted to know why she'd left.

She thought she'd made that perfectly clear.

Men.

She looked up into the bright winter sunlight in time to see Joe dive cleanly into the deep end of the pool. He was a strong swimmer, and before she knew it, he'd surfaced within a few feet of where she stood.

Before she knew what his intention was, he had both her upper arms grasped tightly in his hands. She looked up into his face, and everything she'd feared about meeting him again was in his expression.

Love. Anger. Desire.

She couldn't speak, could only watch the way he studied her face, his eyes meeting hers, then moving to her mouth. She knew he was going to kiss her mere seconds before he did, and she didn't move away from him.

His lips covered hers and all she could think of was how right and good the kiss felt. Safe and familiar. Overwhelming and rawly emotional. She opened her mouth at his first urging, then slid her hands up his powerful chest and linked them around his neck.

He pulled her against him, his hands hot against the small of her back, and through the thin barrier of their swimsuits, she felt the fullness and masculine strength of his arousal.

He caught one of her hands in his and pulled it downward, forcing her fingers to cup his hardness, hold him, acknowledge all that burned between them. And all the time he continued to kiss her, passionate kisses, out-of-control kisses, kisses that let her know that nothing had changed between them, nothing at all.

Her top fell away and her breasts were crushed against his chest. Then his hands caught the bottom of her bikini, and sanity returned full force as he began to strip the last protective bit of clothing off her body.

She broke the kiss, tried to step away. His hand was between her legs, and her face burned at the evidence he discovered there, a wetness, a hotness that was every bit as sexually potent as his full erection.

She wanted him, but she was scared by how much she wanted him. Not now, not this way.

''No,'' she said softly, and it was as if he'd never heard the word. Her bikini bottoms were sliding off, and she dug her nails into his muscular back.

''*No*, Joe! Please!''

That stopped him. Despite all the things she could say about her ex-husband during the end of their relationship, he knew that no, any no, meant no. And he respected her right to that refusal. He'd never forced her in the years they were together.

He'd never had to.

She turned away from him and clumsily tried to pull on the bottom of her swimsuit. It was tangled between her legs, and the water, as well as her trembling fingers, impeded her actions. He probably thought her all sorts of a fool for stopping something that had seemed as passionately inevitable as a sunrise.

But she'd discovered something about herself. She couldn't sleep with Joe, couldn't give that part of herself to him without knowing how he felt about her.

To lose him again would kill her.

HE WATCHED HER, then looked away. Some things were just too intimate. If he'd thought she wouldn't slap his hands away, he would have helped her dress.

Now, bikini bottom in place, she retreated up the stairs. She didn't bother with her top, it had floated to the bottom of the pool. Nina, having had plenty of experience vacationing in Europe, wasn't as self-conscious about being topless as another woman might be.

He watched her, but it wasn't with any form of sexual pleasure. He'd pushed her, too far, too fast. He wouldn't blame her if she simply showered, packed and headed straight back to Los Angeles.

Away from him.

He followed her progress as she grabbed her towel and notepad, then padded back inside the house, shutting the door quietly behind her. Then he climbed out of the pool, sat down on the chaise he'd occupied before, put his head in his hands and wondered how he was ever going to reach the woman he loved.

Chapter Seven

Nice job, Morrissey.

Joe sat out in the garden, Clyde by his side, and watched the sunset. They were always spectacular in Palm Springs, so sudden because the sun went down behind the mountains and it became dark quickly, the way it did in the tropics. You either loved the desert or you hated it, and Joe had fallen in love with it years ago.

He loved the cold, bright weather, and seeing the stars and the moon so very close at night, as if you could reach up and pluck them right out of the sky.

Now the thought of the evening sky brought him absolutely no pleasure at all.

Nina hadn't left yet. He wasn't sure what she was up to, as absolutely no sounds had come from the direction of her bedroom. Now, as he wondered how he could get them talking again after what had happened out in the pool, Joe remembered Robert's entertainment center.

He'd thought of renting all the movies in the John Blackheart series, but he couldn't leave the compound for another twenty-four hours. He *could,* but Robert, Arnie, and especially Nina, might get the wrong idea.

He didn't want that.

But he'd never met an actor yet who wasn't a little bit vain or self-impressed. Or at least obsessed with his work. And Robert Corbin possessed every classic quality an actor had, in abundance.

He'd bet money Robert had all his films, including the Blackheart series. Now it was only a matter of finding them, and asking Sam for a little help in setting up the evening.

She'd just finished taking a shower, then sitting out on the balcony off her bedroom and doing some relaxation and breathing exercises. Since leaving Joe standing in the pool, all she'd tried to do was simply calm down.

Now she stared at her closet and wondered if she had the courage to simply pack her bags and leave.

Oh, she knew the psychological jargon. They'd hurt each other badly, and as a modern-day woman she should be perfectly capable of standing on her own two feet and carving out a fabulous life for herself.

Then why did everything seem a little flat without Joe? Why did she feel her life was simply stalled, that she was waiting for him to come back into it and make it right?

How could she let go of this relationship, after all they'd meant to each other?

She was afraid of getting hurt.

But on the other hand, nothing could hurt as much as not trying.

Maybe if I asked him to go slower...

What they had together was too much. Too passionate, too sexual, and way too successful. They'd been handed the emotional dynamite with which to blow their entire relationship clean out of the water.

She was ashamed of herself. It wasn't as if she were bereft, without the means to support herself. Women left marriages all the time, with children, with little money, all in the name of reclaiming their lives and finding safety and shelter from a relationship that didn't work.

Even divorced, she couldn't seem to let go of him.

She glanced away from the closet, knowing she wasn't going to leave. Not yet. They hadn't even been able to manage twenty-four hours together without a huge conflict. How would they ever get a treatment done for the studio, let alone an entire screenplay?

But that wasn't the question her heart wanted answered.

Why can't we make it work?

Nina sat down on the bed and absently stroked Stan's fur. He and Ollie were absorbed in a game of hide-under-the-bed, and barely noticed her attention.

She'd been so angry at Joe when he hadn't come after her. Angry because she knew, with all her instincts, that he'd spoiled her for any other man. It wasn't possible for any two people to have been as close as they were.

She didn't want anyone else. She never would.

He didn't want her. Oh, he did, but any fool knew you needed more than an incredible sex life to make a marriage work.

She breathed deeply, pleased that her lungs seemed to be working again. That was something, at least. How strange, that she'd driven out here and thought of her stay in the desert as a healing time. Calming. Comfortable.

Words she'd never think of when she thought of Joe.

The knock on the door startled her, but she knew who had to be on the other side before she got up off the bed to answer it.

HE FELT FOOLISH, standing at her door with the flowers he'd had phoned in. Peonies and roses, her favorites. Lush, with full blooms and brilliant colors. Nina loved fresh flowers, she'd had them all over the house they'd rented in Malibu after their second

John Blackheart screenplay sold for an astronomical amount.

He'd liked the way she'd managed their home, though he didn't remember ever telling her. She had a flair for making any space they inhabited beautiful, even the tiny one-bedroom apartment they'd shared in Hollywood.

Now, as she opened the door, he hoped she wouldn't simply stare at him and slam it in his face.

The door opened, and he saw the expression in her eyes as she took him in, flowers in hand, standing in front of her.

"I'm sorry," he said. Words were so inadequate at times, but these were the only ones he knew.

"I am, too."

He sensed she was talking about everything that had transpired between them once it had all started to go so wrong.

"Truce?"

She nodded.

He handed her the flowers. She found a vase in the bathroom and arranged them by her bed. He liked the thought of her seeing them first thing in the morning.

He still stood in the doorway, somewhat unsure of what to do. He didn't want to push her farther than she wanted to go, and he didn't want to invade her territory.

"You can come in," she said, as she arranged the flowers just so.

He walked into the bedroom, then had to smile at the antics of the two younger cats. They were racing around the bed, ambushing each other above and below, grabbing each others necks, biting each other's butts as they play-fought furiously across the room.

"Where's the fat one?"

"He's taking a nap in the bathroom."

This was getting them nowhere fast. He tried again.

"Robert has all the Blackheart movies on video in the other room."

That stilled her hands. The flowers had been perfectly arranged by now, and he realized she was nervous, still fiddling with the brilliant blooms.

"I guess . . . we should watch them."

Her voice sounded sad, and he knew she was remembering other times, other places.

"Would you like to join me?" He decided to make the invitation slightly more formal. It might make her less jumpy around him.

She hesitated, her back still turned toward him.

"I'll keep my hands to myself."

Her hands stilled, then she turned to him.

"It wasn't all your fault, Joe." She hesitated, seemed to be searching for the right words, and he wouldn't have made a sound if his life depended on it.

"Could we...could we just be friends for a while?"

He remembered another part of their relationship, so long ago. A lifetime ago. And he knew Nina needed time as a way of building a certain amount of emotional security.

He'd give her whatever she needed.

"Sure."

She smiled at him, and he knew he'd give her as much time as she needed. Knew he would do anything for this particular woman, because he'd never stopped loving her.

IT WAS HARDER to watch *Deadly Threat* than either of them had imagined.

They sat side by side on the comfortable leather couch, a huge bowl of buttered popcorn in front of them along with two colas and an assortment of candy. Movie food was movie food, after all.

Nina found herself closing her eyes through parts of the film. Especially when the credits rolled at the beginning, when she'd seen "Story and Screenplay by Joe and Nina Morrissey." Her mind had flashed back to that first showing at a real theater, how she'd grabbed his hand, how she'd barely been able to sit in her seat.

How excited they'd been.

Everything they'd ever dreamed had been up on that screen.

Now, halfway through the movie, she couldn't keep her mind on the images on-screen. She kept remembering the little things, like Joe crumpling up pieces of paper and tossing them to her to get her attention. The way he'd grabbed her ankle when she'd crossed the room to sharpen a pencil. The look in his eyes that signaled their working day was over, and it was time to play.

She thought of all the afternoons she'd been stretched out on the rug, reading final copy. And the way he'd touched her, run his fingers over her wrist, captured her hand, rolled over on his back and pulled her on top of him. Slipped his fingers around the back of her neck and brought her lips down to meet his....

The room seemed too hot, and Nina fidgeted in her seat, then glanced over at Joe to see if he was having the same sort of problems.

She couldn't tell.

Every frame, every scene, brought back memories that had nothing to do with the movie they were watching. She thought of all the interviews she'd watched, and how famous celebrities always remarked on the fact that the best years were the struggling years, the passionate years, the years in which they worked so hard to make it to the top.

She'd never known how true that was until this moment.

Toward the end of the film, after John Blackheart had rescued his pregnant wife and the story was winding to its conclusion, she remembered an argument they'd had over children. Joe had been very clear about wanting a family, but she'd been frightened and wanted to wait a little longer.

She wondered if they would have tried harder if they'd had a child.

The sob caught her completely by surprise, bursting up from her soul and into her throat. She covered her face with one hand, ashamed at being so vulnerable in front of him.

But she couldn't stop crying.

SHE WAS EXPRESSING what he felt, and he couldn't let her go through it alone.

Joe moved across the couch and put his arm around his wife. He'd never think of her as his ex, no matter how long he lived. He loved her, and it killed him to see her in such pain.

He turned off the video and let her cry in his arms, in the darkened room. He eased her into his lap and rubbed her back. He kissed the top of her head and wondered how they could have possibly ended up this way.

"Nina, don't—"

"What happened? What happened to us? I don't understand why it went so wrong...."

"Shh." He stroked her back, smoothed her hair off her face, comforted her as best he could.

"I'm so sorry about—about the baby—"

Something inside him went perfectly still.

"The baby you wanted—I should have—given it to you. But I was—selfish—"

"No." He relaxed, realizing what she was talking about. "No. You weren't ready. I knew that."

"I wouldn't have left, then—"

Her words forced him to acknowledge a truth he'd let slip to the back of his mind. He'd never felt good enough for Nina, and a part of him had thought of their having a child as a way to keep her with him. He knew her boundless capacity for love, knew she would make a wonderful mother despite her experiences with her own. But his motives had been selfish, and now they came back and shamed him.

"It wasn't the right time," he whispered, his voice tight. He kissed her forehead, then held her until the crying stopped.

Neither of them was in any mood to see another video.

He walked her to her bedroom door.

"Sleep in. We can start working whenever you get up."

She looked so bedraggled it broke his heart. Nina tonight was a far cry from the gorgeous woman by the pool this afternoon. Now she simply looked tired. Emotionally exhausted.

"Thanks, Joe."

"Hey, my pleas—"

Her arms around him caught him by surprise. She hugged him, hard, then gave him a swift kiss on the cheek before darting inside her bedroom—and locking the door.

He smiled as he walked down the hall.

WORK WAS not going well.

It was nothing he could pin down, but by the time their first ten workdays had passed out by the pool, Joe had to admit to himself that the Morrissey magic had evaporated into thin air.

It was gone. Finished. Kaput.

Their ideas were stale and derivative, their dialogue on the nose. John Blackheart couldn't have been more boring if he'd been an insurance salesman. It was about the only idea they hadn't tried.

And Nina, his wife, was driving him crazy.

He knew the rules. Just friends. She needed time. It made him ashamed of himself that he couldn't keep his sexuality under control for the sake of the work. And he remembered other working arrangements, other times they'd created together.

They'd ended up in bed after almost every work session.

He'd been celibate for almost eighteen months, and not one of those days had been more difficult than the last ten.

The worst thing was, he doubted she had any idea what she was doing to him. Oh, he could try to keep his bodily responses under control, but his mind, that most brilliant and complicated of sexual organs, was going into overdrive.

Daily.

Constantly.

He didn't even want to think about his nights.

And it struck him, with the sudden intensity the truth always possesses, that he wouldn't be able to write a decent line until he got her into bed.

SHE KNEW she'd set limits, and at the time they'd seemed like the right ones. But now, chewing on the end of her pencil, Nina wondered if Joe had any idea of the sensual torment she was going through.

What had worked at age eighteen was absolutely impossible ten years later. For one thing, she hadn't known what she was missing, therefore she hadn't been tempted by it. But once she'd made love with Joe, she'd experienced a pleasure she didn't want to do without.

Each day that passed wound her nerves tighter and tighter. She remembered the way they were together, it was something made palpable when he looked at her, when he accidently touched her—and he did that as little as possible—and even when he spoke to her.

Each move he made, each gesture, brought erotic memories to the forefront of her mind. The sound of his voice brought back memories of other times, other places.

Brought back memories of lying in bed with him and knowing that this was as good as loving ever got.

"Nina, what if he knew the villain from the past—"

That's it, baby. That's good...

"All right, so he's stranded. So what? I don't think this part is that interesting—"

Give it to me, Nina. Give me what I want...

He touched her leg by accident, passing her a sheaf of paper. And she thought of the way he touched the back of her leg while they were joined together, urging it higher so he could go deeper inside her....

She watched him as he studied the electronic prose on the laptop computer screen, and remembered the way he watched her in bed, so intently, as if her every move fascinated him. He'd been so intent, so passionate, so powerfully male—

"I can't do this anymore."

She blinked, then looked at Joe as if seeing him for the first time.

"Can't do what?"

"This." His gesture took in the mess by the pool, a clutter of blue, four-by-six note cards, several pieces of script notes and the three pages of treatment they'd managed to commit to paper thus far.

"It stinks, Nina. None of it works."

"I know."

He was restless, impatient, all pent-up male energy as he looked at her.

"I can't do it, Nina." His voice roughened. "Not with you this close. Not without being with you. Inside you."

He'd voiced her own thoughts, and she sat very still.

He picked up the battery-operated laptop and threw it into the pool.

It made the strangest sound as sparks crackled and it partially exploded. Then she watched as it sank to the bottom.

She felt his fingers close around her ankle, then he was dragging her across her towel toward him, beneath him.

"I can't—" he began.

"I know," she whispered, before she slid her hands along his back, down his spine, under the back of his suit.

He kissed her, roughly, almost violently, and she knew this would not be gentle loving. This would be the physical response to ten days of wanting, needing, fantasizing. This would be a taking, a claiming, a desire that filled both of them so sharply they could think of nothing else.

She hesitated, remembering Sam, Robert's house-man, then felt Joe react to her body's subtle response. Lifting his head from her neck, he glared down at her.

"Don't stop me, Nina."

"But *Sam*," she whispered.

There was a cabana on the far side of the pool, and he picked her up and carried her to its cool shelter. Once they were down among the cushions on the floor, he kissed her as if he were starving, and she responded with just as much need.

She couldn't think, could only feel as he stripped off her bikini, then his own brief suit. Then they were lying together, arms and legs entwined, and he was holding her, kissing her as if he'd never let her go.

Her nipples were hard and aching long before he touched them with his hands and mouth. She reached for him, found him, so hard and hot and smooth in her hands. She stroked him, but he took her hands away and pinned them above her head, then kissed her with a savagery that almost stole her breath away.

She moaned, unintelligible, inarticulate sounds. Then his name, over and over as he slowly moved down her body, tasting her, teasing her, arousing her. First with his fingers, then with his tongue. And she reveled in the power he had over her body. When she opened her eyes and saw him, he was watching her, smiling.

He broke the intimate eye contact, then urged her on to her back and slid between her thighs. He thrust inside her, filling her, moving with such force that she was pushed along the cabana floor among all the pillows with his first, fast strokes.

She grasped his shoulders, then his hair, then arched her back as she reached another sensual peak of excitement. Her response triggered his, she knew he'd already held back too long, then she was flooded with his release, the wettest, sweetest warmth. She trembled as she took that part of him deep inside her, held him tightly in her arms.

He didn't move for a few minutes, and she enjoyed the sensuality of his heavy body pressing her into the cushions. Then he slowly raised his head and looked down at her, and it was as if some of the wildness had left his eyes.

"I'm sorry," he whispered.

"No." She stroked his hair off his forehead. "You needed it, and so did I." She'd decided, during one of the long, lonely nights in her room, that she was never going to lie to Joe again. Denying her feelings had always been her problem, waiting until they built up into an anger that no one could appease.

From this moment on, she was going to be honest with him.

He slid off her, then pulled her tightly against him. A breeze blew in from the outside, cooling the light sheen of sweat on their bodies.

They were quiet for a few minutes, and Nina needed the time to reorient herself. Their relationship had changed in the space of a heartbeat. Joe had taken control again, become their leader, but it was a position she liked having him take.

She felt his hand as he rubbed her back, then cupped her buttocks.

"You've lost weight," he remarked.

"You," she whispered into his neck, "look disgustingly healthy.

He laughed at that, and continued to run his hands over her body, as if starved for the touch of her.

"Was there anyone else?"

She knew what it had cost him to ask that particular question, so she didn't delay her answer.

"No. Never." Her hand stopped its restless movement against his hair-roughened chest. "You?"

"Nope." He kissed her, then rolled them over so she was astride him. Taking a piece of her hair in his fingers, he tweaked it gently. "You should know, lightning never strikes twice."

Her eyes filled, and she lay down on top of him, breathed deeply of that scent that was his alone, letting it comfort her. Somehow, the world had never seemed as frightening a place when she was in Joe's embrace.

"You're still angry with me," he said.

"You became a stranger. Toward the end, I didn't even know who I was living with."

His hand tightened on her hip. "I thought a lot about it, after you left." He rubbed the knuckles of his hand against her cheekbone. "Nina, they were trying to separate us."

"I know they didn't want me in on it. I've never understood that whole thing they had against women writers."

"You scared them."

"Yeah, well what happened to you scared me."

She watched as color flooded his high cheekbones, but he kept a tight grip on her. Almost as if he expected her to run away again.

"It was the money."

"Damn it, Joe, my grandmother never meant—"

"Not that money. The money I felt I had to make for you."

Now she was furious with him, and struggled to get away. He held her tightly, and she knew she couldn't leave him again, she'd have to get to the truth.

"What did I ever do to make you feel you had to be this damn money-making machine?" Her voice was tight and low.

"Nothing."

She stared at him. Of all the replies he could have given her, this one was the least expected.

"Nothing. It was all me. My pride. When I found out what you came from, and then realized what you'd given up to marry me—"

She struggled away from his grip. "I didn't give up a thing I didn't want to give up! Damn it, Joe, let me go!"

"No. This gets settled now. I took what those bastards offered me because I thought that if I played the game the way they wanted it played, even for a short time, I could make enough money to tell them all to go to hell."

Quick, angry tears rose in her eyes as she thought of all the nights she'd remained home. Alone. Frightened by what she saw her husband becoming. Frightened at the thought of losing her writing partner and best friend in the world.

"Well I wish you would have told me what you were up to. I thought you thought I was dragging you down."

His grip on her tightened. "Never."

"How was I supposed to know that, Joe? You were never home."

"I know." He let go of her for an instant, then rolled over so he was above her, pinning her against the soft cushions. "But you never asked, even when I asked what was wrong."

"I couldn't explain how I felt—"

"It's a two-way street, Nina—"

"But you might have left me—"

He lowered his head until his lips were against her ear, then whispered, "I'm not your mother."

She went perfectly still.

"I would have never left you, Nina. Ever. I know why you ran away, so you could leave first. So it would hurt less. So you'd be in control and things wouldn't be as frightening."

She was so angry, so speechless, she could only struggle and try to get away from him.

"How dare you tell me what I was thinking, feeling—"

"I know because I did the same thing. I wanted to be in control. Of the money, of you, of everything."

She went limp against him then, tired of fighting him, tired of all the confusion and heartache both of their deepest fears had put them through.

"Nina," he said softly, gently. "Nina, listen to me a second. Then if you want to leave, I won't stop you."

She didn't want to leave him, and couldn't understand why he would still believe she would.

"I come from nothing. My own father didn't even want to stick around. All I knew about family was what my mother provided, and she did an incredible job. But she couldn't give me my father back, and for a long time I wondered what was wrong with me. Why he left."

"Nothing's wrong with you," she whispered.

"I know that now. I didn't, then. I was a hellish responsibility to my mom, but she stuck by me. I just thought all mothers did that."

"No. You're wrong about that."

"You're right. She stuck by me, even on the night she had to come bail me out of jail."

"What!" He'd never told her that.

"I was running with this gang. I told you, she got me out of that as soon as she could. But not before I'd seen some of the worst my neighborhood had to offer."

She put her hand on his shoulder, offering comfort. Caught up in his story, and slowly coming to realize there was a lot about this man she still didn't know.

"She bailed me out and set me straight. I joined the service because I knew that if I couldn't have a father in the conventional sense, I needed some pretty strict guidance from someone.

"I went to college right after I got out, but I felt different from the other students. Older." He paused. "Flawed."

"No," she said, holding him closer.

"So I graduate and decide to write, and I move into the apartment in Hollywood and I meet you. And yeah, I saw things about you that made me feel you came from a better background, but nothing that made me believe you had the kind of money you sprang on me on our honeymoon."

"Would you have married me if you'd known about the trust fund?" She challenged him directly now, looking into his eyes. Still angry. His grip on her had eased. Nothing could have made her leave.

"No. Not if I'd known. It would have killed me to walk away from you, but I couldn't have messed up your life that way."

"Then I was right not to tell you."

"Why?"

"I knew once you married me, you'd never walk away from your responsibilities."

He closed his eyes and leaned his head back. They'd shifted positions again, and were lying side by side on the floor of the cabana.

"I wanted you," she continued shakily, "like I've wanted nothing else in my entire life. And I didn't want you to leave."

He took her hand in his and simply linked their fingers, held her tightly.

"I was wrong, Nina. About the money, about what it represented. I just—I grew up around a lot of men who didn't take their responsibilities seriously, who let their women support them. I didn't want to take so much away from you—"

She put a finger against his lips, stopping him in midsentence. "Do you remember that last argument? What I said?"

He smiled.

"Joe, you never took anything away from me. You gave to me, all the time, endlessly. No one had ever done that for me before, except my grandmother. When I lost her, I thought that part of my life was all over. I tried giving to my mother and Brad, but all they did was take.

"Then I met you, and you were so confident, so sure of yourself. I'd never heard anyone who had the guts to say, 'I'm going to write a screenplay.' Just like that. I thought it was a miracle. I wanted to be like you."

"It was all for show. A big bluff." He took a deep breath, and she could feel him trying to release emotional tension. "Because I never thought I could do it, until we started working together."

"But you finished that first one long before I met you!"

"But it wasn't any good." He rolled to his side, then leaned on his elbow as he looked down at her. "The first time I saw you, I—that lightning, it hit me right between the eyes. Right in my heart. Everything else was a bonus. The night I came up to your room and saw all the books, I thought, maybe I can talk to her about it, what I want to do, where the problems are.

"After that first night, when you invited me up, I knew I was never going to leave.

"I can't write without you, Nina. I don't want to. So maybe I had all the bluffing ability, and I could talk a good show. But you were the one who steadied me, who put the heart and soul into everything we ever wrote."

"Stop." She kissed him. "I feel exactly the same way about you. I've always thought I just kind of skimmed along with you, hanging on, trying to catch up."

He shook his head. They lay silently next to each other for almost a minute before Joe spoke.

"I tried to tell them all that. At that meeting at Robert's beach house. They didn't get it. They didn't *want* to get it. They never thought you were really a partner."

"I know." It hurt to remember, but felt good at the same time. Like opening a wound that was festering, poisoning your blood, and finally letting it begin to heal.

"I never felt that way, Nina."

"For a while, I thought you did."

"No. Never."

She looked up at him and caught the exact moment when his eyes darkened. When he began to study her with that intent, frankly sexual manner that let her know their sensual afternoon was far from over.

He moved over her, covering her body with his own. She felt his arousal against her skin, hard and smooth and so warm. Her arms came up around him, she opened her legs to cradle him more securely. He took his weight on his elbows as he kissed her. Then, their faces mere inches apart, he whispered, "Who do you really think is in control here?"

She shook her head, not caring, then slid her hand up into the softness of his hair.

He lowered his head to her breasts and she cried out, softly, as he took one nipple into his mouth and pulled on it with his teeth.

"Who?"

"You are," she whispered, her head falling back, her eyes tightly shut.

He laughed, low in his throat. "I don't think so." She felt his hand find her, cup her, then open her with his fingers. She moaned as he began to arouse her, with soft, seductive strokes.

"You think—I—am?" She could barely get the words out, she was so excited by what he was doing to her.

He took his hand away and slowly began to enter her, filling her, stretching her, making her moan low in her throat.

"You are. You know you are, the way you make me feel. The way you make me want you. I was useless out there, all I could think of was getting inside you, everything I wanted to do to you."

She caught her breath, then shut her eyes against the intensity of his gaze, her feelings.

"I wanted this, Nina. I can't live without it. This is what they mean when they talk about lightning striking your heart. This."

He was completely sheathed inside her now, but not moving, simply lying on top of her and pinning her to the cabana floor. She couldn't have moved if her life depended on it.

She wouldn't have wanted to.

"Open your eyes."

She did.

"I missed this."

She tried to speak. He moved slightly, and the words caught in the back of her throat.

"Did you miss it, Nina?"

"Yes...."

He lowered his lips to her ear, kissed the side of her neck, then whispered, "I love being inside you."

He hadn't moved at all, but his words caused small, involuntary feminine contractions. She felt his body tense, and lay perfectly still beneath him.

"I love what you do to me," she whispered. "I missed it so much."

"Mmm." He began to move, long, slow, deep strokes meant to arouse. He took his time with her, and while their first coupling had been urgent, almost frantic, this time he made love to her as if their mutual pleasure was his only concern in the world. The only thing he wanted to do.

"You'll move into my bedroom tonight," he whispered as he held her on the brink of an almost painful arousal.

"Yes," she whispered, her face buried against his neck.

"I'm never letting you go again."

She cried out, digging her nails into his strong back.

"You belong to me, Nina."

Lying next to him as the late-afternoon breezes washed over their naked bodies, Nina felt contentment down to that deep soul level that can't be explained. She knew their lovemaking had been inevitable, they'd been on a collision course with it from the moment they'd seen each other again.

Now, sexually sated and relaxed, she didn't want to think about their problems. She decided to take this time with Joe, and the rest of the world be damned. The screenplay, too. If they could continue to talk like they had this afternoon, there might be some hope for their relationship after all.

Chapter Eight

She moved into his bedroom that same night.

They didn't talk much. There wasn't a whole lot to move. Nina had the strangest feeling in the pit of her stomach, seeing her clothes next to Joe's in the closet, her things next to his in the bathroom.

Her heart knew they were doing the right thing. Her head, ever-cautious, wasn't as sure.

Even the cats moved in with Joe. As all three got along with Clyde, and he adored them, there was no problem with their pets sharing the same space.

They'd taken a shower together in the cabana, then pulled on their bathing suits and headed back to the main house. After getting dressed and moving her things, Joe left, telling her he had to talk to Sam.

Nina, exhausted, stretched out on the king-size bed they were going to share.

She felt so open and vulnerable after making love with Joe, but also free. The tension that had been building between them was gone, though if she remembered her ex-husband's sexual rhythm, he'd make love to her this evening, as well.

Closing her eyes, she placed a hand on her lower abdomen and tried to relax as she breathed. She wanted to keep up with Joe, she didn't want to worry him with the fact that she was still getting over a bad case of pneumonia.

She'd overdone it today, and that was that.

Her doctor had warned her. Some days she felt terrific, some days she could barely drag herself out of bed. She'd been so excited this afternoon, had wanted to make love to Joe so badly, and now she was paying the price.

Throughout her entire illness, she'd felt as if she was taking one step forward, another back. Then a few more back, and another cautious step forward. It was the most frightening thing in the world, to feel your lungs closing up and realize you couldn't breathe.

Though she would have hated not having Joe's company at the compound, and knew the only way they were going to do John Blackheart justice was if they wrote his last adventure together, a small part of her still wished she'd had this time alone.

So much for rest, relaxation and recuperation.

She knew Joe would be upset if he found out she was keeping something so crucial from him. She'd also resolved not to have any more secrets between them. But the last thing she wanted him to do was look upon her as some sort of charity case.

She closed her eyes, and as she drifted off to sleep, felt Ollie come up and lie down behind her head, snuggled next to her on the pillow.

WHEN HE CAME BACK into the bedroom, he smiled at the sight that greeted him.

Nina, fast asleep on his bed, with all three cats cuddled close. Ollie at her head, Henry curled up by her side, and Stan covering her feet. Clyde was stretched out full-length at the very bottom of the bed, and the only way Joe would have realized the basset hound was even alive was the slight wrinkling of his loose forehead skin as he acknowledged his master's presence.

Sam had turned the heater on, as winter evenings in the desert could be quite cold. The sun was setting, and his bedroom had the same incredible view of the Coachella Valley that Nina's did.

Joe studied her as she slept. Her color wasn't good, she looked tired in a peculiar way. The way people looked right before they dropped.

Something else is going on here.

He wasn't going to push. Their encounter by the cabana had been enough. For now. She was back in his bed, and they'd started dealing with all the confusion and bitterness that had poisoned their marriage and caused their divorce.

He just hoped she wouldn't be too angry that he'd never divorced her.

Picking up the phone receiver, he placed a call to the kitchen.

"Can you hold dinner for a while, Sam?" he asked, keeping his voice low and his gaze on his wife.

"Certainly, sir. Just ring me when you'd like to begin your meal."

He hung up the phone, then sat down in a chair that afforded him an incredible view. The real world could cease to exist if a person spent enough time in a place like Palm Springs. It was a world of swimming pools and sun worshipers, golf courses and endless sunshine, with a number of celebrities thrown in for good measure.

The people in the desert had managed to keep the city under control, with no high rises and neon signs. It still had a rather charming, small-town feel, and Joe liked that. The entire area was a green oasis, a desert jewel, far away from the insanity that was the state of mind called Hollywood. Shielded from the rest of the world by a ring of mountains, it was the perfect place to find a little bit of peace.

Robert Corbin had been wise to locate one of his homes here.

They'd been lucky this time. Both he and Nina had found a sanctuary, a place to heal their emotional wounds. He knew Arnie had arranged their meeting, and he wondered if his friend and agent had hoped something more than a screenplay would come of it.

Nina murmured softly in her sleep, then turned. All three cats compensated, adjusting their furry bodies. Clyde simply snored on.

Joe knew he wasn't at his best when it came to talking things through. He was a man who felt more comfortable with action than words, except when writing. Now, content in the knowledge that he'd literally pulled Nina closer to him, he sat and watched the brief sunset blaze color over the city spread out below.

SHE WOKE UP, disoriented at first, to find Joe lying next to her. He was wearing a pair of jeans, had discarded his shirt and was reading the trades. He'd also covered her with one of the throws at the foot of the large bed.

"Hi," she said, wondering how she could suddenly feel so self-conscious about the erotic afternoon they'd shared. There was nothing they hadn't explored sexually, he probably knew her body better than his own.

"Good nap?"

She nodded. She felt better. Stronger. Ready to face whatever was thrown at them.

"Hungry?"

Joe was a Latin at heart, always taking care of people. His mother had instilled that warmth in him, that caring that transcended any masculine stereotype. He'd always cared for her, even when it had seemed he was doing exactly the opposite.

"I could eat."

"Good."

He picked up the phone and spoke with Sam, then brought his attention back to her.

"Robert called while you were asleep."

"Yeah?"

"He asked how things were going. I convinced him we were doing fine."

"Did he have any ideas?"

Joe laughed, and Nina couldn't suppress a grin. It was so strange, how no one wanted to stick with the thing they did the most competently. Actors wanted to direct or write. Directors wouldn't rest until they were producers. And anyone, at any given time, could be counted on to be "working on a screenplay."

Though Robert hadn't changed much in the three action-adventure scripts they'd written for him, he still fancied himself something of a writer and was constantly coming up with ideas they could "incorporate into the story."

"I'm sorry I asked," she said.

"No, you'll love this one. He asked me if there was any way we could put John on a nuclear submarine."

Nina started to laugh then, lying back down on the bed and giving in to the ridiculousness of the suggestion.

"Why, does his current girlfriend have a thing for subs?"

"That's not all."

"Oh God, I don't know if I can take it."

"This was what he said. 'What if John Blackheart found himself stranded on a submarine, then notices that it's *going the wrong way*. Okay? Okay? Whad'ya think of that one? Good, huh?'" His impression of Robert Corbin was wickedly accurate, and Nina dissolved into another fit of giggles.

"Wait, wait. Now, where was this sub going in the first place? And how did John get aboard?"

Joe waved his hand, mimicking the star's physical movements. "'Details, details. Hey, that's what we're paying you guys all that money to come up with. Okay? Okay?'"

"I hope that was it."

"Not quite."

She piled some pillows against the headboard and sat up.

"Tell me the worst."

"He thinks that this time John should have a dog."

"A *dog?* In an action-adventure movie? What is this, *Turner and Hootch Are Above the Law?* Or maybe Lassie could try to get the miner out of a radioactive mine shaft filled with Nazis! What is he, nuts?"

"Now it wasn't my idea. I didn't encourage him—"

"And where's the poor thing going to exercise on a submarine?"

Joe could barely contain his laughter.

"And not just any dog. 'Not one of those little, annoying poodles or anything like that. I want John to have a wonder dog, a German shepherd or a rottweiler.' "

"Do the producers know about this?"

"I have a feeling they do."

"I am *not* giving John Blackheart a dog. The way these guys work, the dog would end up with a bigger part than his wife, who I think we should bring back. I was thinking—"

"Yeah?"

"I say we totally ignore the fourth film and continue from the third. This is the movies, after all, and we can just pretend that his horrible divorce never happened. I hated that actress, she was just there to add a little T and A to a script that should've never been produced in the first place. What the hell was Robert thinking of?"

"Naps do wonders for your disposition."

"Well, what do you think?"

"I'm with you. I've been writing myself into corners, thinking of how to correct everything that was wrong with that last Blackheart film. I think if we even start to try, we'll spend the whole first act, and maybe part of the second, apologizing."

"Forget that. Let's just open with a big explosion or something with action—"

"A car chase—"

"An earthquake—"

"Total, citywide anarchy—"

"Someone could have put together a nuclear missile, or maybe a terrorist android—"

"No, a nuclear submarine—"

"Manned by an evil superdog!"

They were both still laughing when Sam brought in their dinner.

DINNER WAS superb.

It had been an inspiration on Joe's part, to celebrate their renewed collaboration with prime rib and scampi. Even Henry had been allowed one garlicky shrimp, which he promptly devoured. Ollie was using his as a hockey puck, while Stan stared longingly at a piece of meat on Joe's plate and Clyde retired to the kitchen for a large beef bone.

"We could put Henry on the sub, but it would sink."

"Joe, that's cruel."

Henry, hearing his name, meowed happily.

"Nah, it wouldn't work. They'd need a wide-angle lens."

"Joe, he's really trying, and remarks like that don't make a diet any easier."

Joe simply laughed. "If we can't come up with any ideas that are better than these, we should give it up right now."

The phone rang halfway through dessert, and Joe answered.

"Hey, Arnie. No, she's right here. Yeah. Yeah. Oh, yeah. No. No submarine. I want you to put that in the contract. And no dog."

He handed the phone to Nina.

"How are you?" Arnie sounded so pleased that she and Joe were talking, Nina couldn't find it in her heart to be mad at him. Grateful, yes. Mad, no.

"Fine. I think we can come up with a story to top the first three, but we're planning on just ignoring the fourth installment."

"That sounds wise."

"Can you do anything to head Robert off at the pass? Those ideas of his..."

"He's flying up to Pebble Beach for a golf tournament in two days, I think that should distract him for at least a week."

They chatted a bit, then she handed the phone back to Joe.

"I think we need a few days to rest before we get into the script. We've been going around and around, getting nowhere, and we just need some time to hang out and refill the well, you know?"

He laughed at something that Arnie said, then replied, "Yeah, you too. No, anytime. One of us should be up. Fine."

When he hung up the phone, she feigned innocence.

"What? No mention of Lassie?"

"I think that we should get out of here for a while. Go to the movies, go shopping, pick up some books and magazines, anything to get our brains jumpstarted."

"Okay."

"Why don't we sleep in again, then go to the mall tomorrow and see what's playing?"

She knew it was important for a screenwriter to keep current, but more than that, she looked forward to spending an uncomplicated day with Joe.

"Sounds good."

They finished their dinner, then Sam cleared the table and presented dessert. Vanilla ice cream rolled in toasted coconut and drowned in homemade chocolate sauce.

She ate every last bit.

"I like seeing you eat," Joe remarked. "You've lost too much weight."

She wagged her finger at him. "Mr. Bossy."

He grinned. "Not that I don't like what I see...."

He didn't approach her that evening, simply kissed her good-night. Then he reached for the novel he was reading and turned on the reading lamp by his side of the bed.

She closed her eyes, snuggling down into expensive sheets and enjoying the pleasant tiredness that settled over her. She liked sleeping in the same bed as Joe, it was comforting to have him near.

She'd had a long and trying day, and could do with a good night's sleep. Knowing Joe, he'd find a way to wake her up in the morning.

SHE COULDN'T breathe.

Nina eased herself up in the large bed, then tried propping more pillows beneath her. It didn't help that much, and she knew she was in for a long night. The room was dark and absolutely silent.

She coughed, and not wanting to wake Joe, she went into the bathroom. She turned on the shower, letting warm steam fill the huge room. She was searching through a drawer for her inhaler when Joe found her.

Within fifteen minutes, she was breathing a little more normally.

Robert's master bathroom was huge, almost like a salon that just happened to have a monstrously large bathtub in the middle of it. Now, Nina sat in one of the comfortable chairs, hardly daring to meet Joe's eyes.

"Don't you think this is something I should know about?" He wasn't angry with her, and somehow that made her feel even worse. Slowly, haltingly, she told him of the pneumonia and her long recuperation.

"You should've called me."

"Why? I remember your telling me you never wanted to see me again."

"Words, Nina. Angry words. They don't mean anything compared to something like this."

He ran them a hot bath, and got inside the giant tub with her, letting her breathe in more steam.

His back was up against one side of the tub, and he sat her in front of him, between his legs. His actions weren't remotely sexual, he simply helped her relax her tense muscles.

She leaned against his body, wishing she could borrow just the smallest bit of his strength. Joe had always had an excess amount of energy, and she could have used some of it right about now.

"You know," he said, while the hot water lapped around their bodies and the eucalyptus-scented steam drifted into the air, "I thought about you the moment I saw this bathroom. Even before I knew you were here."

"You did?"

"Yeah. I thought of all the other baths we used to take together."

She smiled, then reached back and tugged his hair.

"How could you have let me push you so hard today?"

She knew how guilty he had to feel about that, and sought to reassure him.

"It wasn't your fault. I'm a big girl."

"I never would have pushed you—"

"I know."

They sat in the steaming tub for almost forty-five minutes, then Nina let the water slowly drain out. The bathtub was the size of a large hot tub, and it took a while for all the water to empty out.

He dried her off with one of the large bath sheets, and caringly lifted her in his arms. He sat in one of the huge, overstuffed chairs, with her cradled in his lap.

And that's where the warm desert sun found them in the morning.

THE PALM DESERT Town Center was unique among malls because it had a skating rink right in the middle, by the movie theater. Before they bought their tickets, they watched as mobs of little boys and girls whizzed over the ice, laughing and shouting.

They had lunch at Hamburger Hamlet, then settled into a movie marathon.

Nina couldn't believe how much she'd missed going to the movies with Joe. At times like this, it felt to Nina as if they were slipping back into their past.

They saw two movies, back-to-back, and would have gone for a third if Joe hadn't been in such an overprotective mood. He ushered her into his

Mercedes, then drove them back to the compound and insisted she take a long nap.

"Damn it, Joe, I'm not an invalid!"

"You need rest."

Everything ground to a halt. He called Arnie, and insisted they have extra time.

"Just give them some cock-and-bull story about how genius can't be rushed. I'll try to have something cooked up by the end of next week. I can talk to them over the speakerphone and buy us some time."

She hated slowing them down. It had been one of her greatest fears before, that she was dragging Joe down with her. Now, she wondered if they would both be better off if he went on with the project by himself.

She broached the subject to him one evening.

"Nope. Forget it. Put it out of your mind."

It was just like him, to be so stubborn.

"This could go on for a long time, Joe."

"We'll work around it. Just rest."

THE DYNAMIC of their relationship had been changed.

Their days were quiet. Joe made sure she napped every day, whenever she felt the slightest bit tired. The cats loved the fact that they spent so much time in bed, and curled around her like a protective shield.

Henry and Stan fell totally in love with Joe, though Ollie remained stubbornly hers. Clyde, shy and easily spooked, slept at the foot of their bed each night, and Nina knew the basset hound was becoming used to her. Joe took over the details of Henry's diet, even running up and down the long hall with the cat and his drag-a-mouse toy and making sure he exercised.

He brushed Ollie's tangled coat every morning and gave him his required Q-Tip to play with. He coaxed Stan out of hiding and was always affectionate with the shy little cat. He loved her animals the way she did and it felt so good to know he was there, and that she could lean on him.

This was what she'd missed when she'd been sick alone. Her husband's calm, comforting presence. Nothing was quite as bad with Joe around. He was calm and collected, and steady as a rock. She knew she could depend on him for anything, and realized that was one of her definitions of love.

He mothered her, and for a woman who had never really known her own mother's love, that was as potent an aphrodisiac as anything she could think of. He nurtured her, protected her.

Over the two weeks he forced her to rest, she grew to love him in a way that was deeper than anything she'd previously experienced, surpassing anything she had ever felt for another human being. And she came to see that what they'd fought over before really had no true power over them in the end.

Careers, money and power weren't a stronger force than love. She would have known all this, had she been listening to her heart instead of her fears.

Had she been listening to her soul, and its needs.

And as she lay in bed and dreamed, Nina began to hope for a future. She also began to intuitively feel the theme of their screenplay, that perhaps it could have something to do with the power of love, and two ordinary people whose emotions for each other triumph over terrible odds.

She and Joe had both liked the actress who had played John Blackheart's wife, but she had been canned when the new writers had come in and taken over. The story line during the fourth film had told of their divorce and her death. She'd been tortured by terrorists, as had their daughter.

Nina would never forgive the writers, three young men in their twenties fresh out of film school, for that little tale. For blithely and violently killing off two characters she and Joe had created and made come alive. She would have respected them more if they'd decided to let John Blackheart follow one of the trends of the nineties, divorcing his wife and replacing her with the bimbo, trophy wife.

But she knew they could fix it, and make the Blackheart family come alive again on-screen.

As she lay in bed and surrendered herself to Joe's care, she realized that so much of what she'd put into John Blackheart's character had been based on Joe. Brad would have soured her on men forever if she hadn't met Joe. And she wondered at her instincts, at her decision to move to Hollywood. It was almost as if fate had put her in the right place at the right time.

As if she and Joe had been destined to meet.

Robert sent them another laptop computer, after Joe told the star that the other had ''accidentally'' fallen into the swimming pool. Joe propped it on his legs in the morning when they sat by the pool, and in the afternoons when they retired to the bedroom. He worked with it on the large bed, right next to her. If she was awake, he asked her questions. If not, he jotted down notes and asked her when she woke up.

It was a comfortable, cosy way of working, and it reminded her of the very first time they'd started to work together. In a way, it had been more fun then. They hadn't been aware of the realities awaiting them. Anything was possible. The story could take off any which way.

Now, that same sense of hope filled Nina, and she prayed they would be able to recapture and nurture their newfound relationship, and not be destroyed by what they'd find back in Los Angeles.

Joe took her to a doctor in Rancho Mirage, who, after conferring with her doctor in Los Angeles, said she was improving.

They celebrated that evening, going out to Lyon's English Grille on Palm Canyon Drive. The prime rib was excellent, and they finished their meal with sherry trifle and cappuccino.

"Italian coffee in an English restaurant," she said as they were getting ready to leave. She liked the restaurant, she and Joe had eaten there before. It was decorated to recreate the atmosphere of an eighteenth-century public eating house.

Once home, she went straight to their bedroom, but didn't fall asleep until Joe came to bed.

She snuggled up against him, then whispered, "I think you'd make a wonderful father."

He knew what she was telling him.

"Not right now, Nina. I talked to the doctor, and he agreed it might be best if we ... took it easy."

She stared at him for a moment, unsure whether she understood.

"No sex? We can't make love?"

"Not for another week. He'll check you then, and if you've made the same sort of improvement, then we can ... resume relations, as he said. But he'd like to see you in excellent health for about a year before we even consider a pregnancy."

"You asked him all this?" She could feel herself beginning to smile, melting inside at the thought that Joe was planning ahead for the two of them.

"Sure. He thought I was your husband."

"You are," she whispered, bringing his hand to her lips, kissing his fingers and remembering when they'd been bruised and bloody from fighting. This was a man who would fight his own battles, and hers, as well. He'd been as strong as it was possible to be, but both of them had stumbled a bit in the face of personal demons.

"You're the only one I ever wanted."

SHE CAME AWAKE from a deep sleep that night, simply opened her eyes and remained perfectly still. She knew exactly where she was, there wasn't a bit of confusion to muddle her brain. And she remembered exactly what had just flitted through her subconscious.

Weather Mountain.

Joe was sleeping soundly beside her, but she knew he wouldn't mind if she woke him up. Not for this.

Only another writer would understand.

She touched his shoulder. She whispered his name. He came awake instantly. Then she wondered why she was whispering, when they were completely alone in the east wing of Robert's huge house.

"I have an idea."

He smiled. The ideas that woke one up out of a sound sleep were usually solid gold.

"Remember when we were plotting the second John Blackheart story and you mentioned that place? Weather Mountain."

He caught her excitement immediately.

"We could trap John inside," she went on. "With his wife. She could be pregnant again, it wouldn't be unreasonable. And they could be with the president, so it could be for both his family *and* love of country—"

But Joe was already firing up the laptop, she could see the pure excitement in his expression from the gentle glow of the liquid crystal screen.

Weather Mountain. It would work. It was the sort of big, sweeping idea a screenwriter prays of getting, and the beauty of this one was that they'd thought of it before and discarded it. Wanted to save it for later, to end the series with, it was that spectacular.

"Baby," Joe said as he began to type, "we're back in business."

Chapter Nine

Weather Mountain.

The president of the United State's personal compound, an entire city built into an actual mountain and capable of withstanding a full-out nuclear attack. In case of such an emergency, it was where the president and his family, as well as key members of his staff, would escape to.

Weather Mountain. Only their idea had put a giant twist on it. The president and some of his staff, along with John Blackheart's wife, would be inside the structure. One of the members of this particular party was a government agent who had turned traitor—who had a nuclear bomb hidden somewhere inside the mountain.

And planned to detonate it, as soon as he had the president and his key people locked inside. This villain's mind was sick and twisted, believing he alone could cleanse the world of evil in a blaze of nuclear fire.

If Weather Mountain could withstand a nuclear blast, it could certainly contain one. Or, more importantly, people would suspend belief and believe that it could. And, of course, John Blackheart would be locked in at the last minute. He would have found out about this traitor and be in the process of trying to get word to the president.

His wife, a respected reporter—and twelve weeks pregnant with their second child—would have been covering the Washington beat, and would have been asked along to tour the intricate complex at the last moment. And best of all, they could tie in this particular traitor-villain with the first film, making his total destruction of this small group of people deep inside the mountain highly personal.

He would want Blackheart himself, in a very emotional, vengeful vendetta. And, as always, it would take every bit of skill their protagonist possessed to get out of this one. Their villain would want to confront Blackheart himself, and kill his wife in front of him in order to see him suffer.

And that would be the only thing delaying the explosion, as the two men played a ruthless game of cat and mouse, outfoxing each other through the endless tunnels, mazes and corridors.

"Sort of like *Alien* meets *Die Hard*," Joe said cheerfully the next morning as he reached for another cup of hot coffee. "The compound could be made up to look a lot like that spaceship in *Alien*."

They'd been up all night, madly typing notes, so excited neither could sleep. It was a good idea, an old idea they'd had years ago, and it had had plenty of time to cook in both their brains.

"What about the daughter?"

"Too much for the audience to worry about. Let's send her off to summer camp."

"Joe, why would the president ask Mrs. Blackheart to come along?"

"Maybe he's heading up a summit meeting on terrorism, and wants to know how she escaped from that deranged group of punks."

"Perfect! I love it! It'll be like our private joke, a real zinger to the last writers. Could we give those terrorists their names? I'd like to rub their snotty little faces in the fact that she survived that dumb idea."

"I don't suppose the dog can come along—"

"I don't think so, Joe."

"Then no sub, either?"

"Unless they order in fast food, no."

"But if the bomb went off—"

"They'd be nuclear subs. I'm sure that would thrill Robert."

"What it would do is get us fired."

"Get back to work, you."

They plotted far into the night, arguing and second-guessing each other until Joe finally called it a day. Nina hadn't even gotten out of her sleepshirt, they'd simply worked out of the bedroom all day, with Sam stopping by periodically to supply them with food.

They had their idea, and it was a killer. They could afford to rest tomorrow, for they'd easily done three days' work in one. As Nina fell asleep, she knew they'd finally hit on the perfect story with which to let John Blackheart go.

WITHIN THE WEEK, they had a rough treatment. They read it to Arnie over the phone, he suggested some excellent changes, which were incorporated.

Confident that they had the beginnings of what they were going to show the studio, they started coaching each other on their pitch.

It wasn't an ordinary pitch, like the frantic sessions they'd done in the beginning of their career. This was a requested pitch, and as such, they had a little more time to prepare. Still, it had to be exciting, and there could be no wasted words or dead spots.

They practiced out by the pool, sometimes getting so carried away and animated that Clyde would wake up and start barking as if to say, "Quiet down! You're ruining my nap!"

Nina went for her follow-up checkup, and the doctor was pleased with her progress.

"'You can resume sexual relations, but with care,'" she quoted to Joe as he drove her back to the compound. "What does that mean, exactly?"

"It means we don't have any fun. No howling at the moon, no going wild, no—"

"Then why do it?"

He glanced her way and grinned, his expression devilish. "We have ways, Nina. We have ways."

HE ASKED Sam to turn the heat up in the indoor pool, and invited her out to the enclosed room for a midnight snack.

Sam had surpassed all other dessert attempts with a concoction called "chocolate decadence." Chocolate cake, rich chocolate filling and a satiny chocolate glaze over all.

Joe also had an expensive bottle of champagne on ice.

The table by the far end of the pool was filled with candles and flowers, and had been transformed into a sort of fairy wonderland. Two places had been set, and as Nina walked into the humid room, she cried out with pleasure at the sight.

"You deserved it, putting up with me in the part of Nurse Ratched."

"You weren't that bad."

They sat at the table by the pool, ate dessert and drank champagne. And talked. And talked some more. It always amazed Nina, how she never ran out of things to talk about with Joe, how he always came up with something that stimulated or delighted her.

"What if—what if they don't want me around for the actual pitch? Like last time?" They might be going up against the same men who had believed her incapable of being a true collaborator.

"Nina, don't worry. I'm going to fix this. We're going to be together, and nothing will come between us again."

She wanted to believe him, but she knew what a hard-hearted town Hollywood could be. The industry could be cruel and unforgiving, and she'd never quite gotten good enough at playing the game.

Sam served them coffee later in the evening, then cleared the table and retired for the night. Now, sitting beside Joe, Nina had a few tricks of her own in store for him.

"Feel like swimming?" she asked.

"Yeah."

They'd both been wrapped in white terry-cloth robes, and now Joe shrugged his off, revealing the skimpy black swimsuit he usually wore. Nina had gone along with his suggestion that they wear their suits out to the pool—to a point.

"Oh, we were supposed to wear our suits?" she asked with exaggerated innocence, slipping her robe off her shoulders. She was completely naked beneath it, and now ran to the deep end of the pool and dived in.

He was right behind her, a strong swimmer, and caught her easily.

"What happened to 'with care'?"

She looked up at him, treading water all the while. His dark eyes were fringed with wet, spiky lashes, his body felt warm to her touch. She let him hold her in the circle of his arms, all the while running her fingers over his chest.

"I've never wanted to be careful with you."

He started swimming toward the shallow end, keeping her in his grasp, until his feet touched bottom and he began walking toward the stairs.

"Put me down!" she cried out, struggling playfully. "You know what the doctor said about my delicate condition."

"Too late." He carried her up the stairs, slung over his shoulder, then walked toward the far end of the glass-enclosed room, where Robert had arranged a profusion of plants that looked as if they belonged in a tropical rain forest. In the middle of all this was a large couch, with curtains, an enchanted bower out of some sort of fairy tale.

Nina caught her breath as Joe set her down on the soft cushions, then lay down beside her.

"How do you feel?"

In answer, she linked her arms around his neck and urged his lips close to hers.

"Getting a little aggressive, aren't we?" he said, when their faces were mere inches apart.

"Oh, you love it."

"Considering how ill you've been, I thought we might play a little game of doctor."

"Doctor?"

"Sure. Didn't you ever play it as a kid?"

"I don't think so."

"Well, it's never too late for childish pursuits. Just trust me, Nina—"

"Said the spider to the fly." But she laughed up at him, and gave him permission. The idea intrigued her. She and Joe had never shied away from indulging their active love of fantasy, and this one sounded fascinating.

"Where's your white coat?"

"It's a nudist hospital."

"Oh, very funny. I suppose you don't have a stethoscope, either."

"Had I suspected your penchant for details, I would have stopped off at a medical supply store."

"No, this is fine. I don't think I want things to get that realistic."

"Now, Nina," he said, trying not to laugh. "Tell me where it hurts."

"Hmm . . ." She looked up at him and decided to play. "I've been feeling so funny, Doctor, all restless and unsettled. It might be my heart."

She took his hand and placed it over her left breast.

"You do have a rather elevated heartbeat." He caressed her soft skin, then pinched her nipple gently until it peaked in response.

"Let me get a closer look," he whispered, then lowered his head and took the tip of her aching breast into his mouth.

She closed her eyes and simply enjoyed his touch, feeling the softness of the cushions behind her back, the moist warmth of the room, the clean smell of green plants.

And his mouth, hot and wet and so knowing. He knew the way she liked to be touched.

"I think I'd better examine the other one," he whispered, and she felt him shift his weight so he was lying on top of her, pressing her down into the soft pillows, holding her tightly against him.

He aroused her to the point of total frustration, then slid up her body and kissed her. She responded wildly, her arms around his waist, her fingers sliding down and caressing his buttocks.

"Don't make me wait," she whispered. "I missed you so much."

He urged her legs apart, and even in the midst of such strong, sexual feeling, she couldn't resist one more joke.

"Why, doctor, that's quite an impressive instrument you have there—"

She broke up, laughing until tears came to her eyes. He caught her silliness, and they lay on the sofa and laughed until their stomachs ached.

"Oh, God, it was that chocolate delight, or whatever it was," Nina said, pressing her hand against her belly. "I shouldn't have eaten so much."

"Tonight," he whispered, "is a night for excess."

"Easy for you to say, when you don't have to take care."

He grinned, and she loved the life she saw shining in his dark eyes. "I'll take care of you."

He sat up, leaning against the back of the couch. Gripping her waist with his hands, he guided her into his lap and slowly lowered her onto him.

His eyes darkened and his fingers tightened over her hips, holding her sharply against him, filling her with him. She closed her eyes and leaned against his chest, then rocked back and forth, gently, so gently.

"It's not howling at the moon," she whispered, "but this comes in a pretty close second."

"We've got plenty of time for that, Nina. All the time in the world."

She believed him.

THEY MADE LOVE every single night after that, and though it might have been gentle, it was never without passion. Nina caught Joe looking at her at odd moments during their working day, and she wondered if they would end up getting married again or simply live together for a while.

Whatever happened, just being with him would be enough.

They set the date for their pitch after conferring with Arnie, and worked like demons to make sure everything came together.

She was still amazed at how different they were as writers. While she worked almost entirely on instinct and faith, Joe counted largely on personal experience. This difference had led to several arguments in the past, and it was exactly the same with this script.

"Wait, this guy disables the car so it can go so far and no farther? Nina, how exactly is that possible?"

"I'm not sure, but there has to be some way of doing it. They're always doing it on the soaps."

"That's cutting the brake lines, so that by the time they've sped up, the car's totally out of control."

"But it makes sense—"

"How would it be done?"

"I don't know! We could call a garage."

"Maybe I'll do a little experimenting with my car," he said.

"Leave mine alone!" she replied.

THAT EVENING, there was a thunderstorm.

They stood out on the balcony, watching the violent rain travel swiftly over the valley floor, seeing electric forks of lightning flash, sparkle and touch down in the distance, hearing the rumble of thunder.

Toasty warm inside one of Joe's sweatshirts, Nina leaned into the cool breeze and breathed deeply. She loved the way the desert smelled before a storm, and tonight the air was fragrant with that damp green smell, and filled with a sizzling tension.

The lightning came closer, and still they sat out on the balcony, wanting to watch until the last possible moment.

"*Coup de foudre*," she said softly. "I never wanted to fight it."

"I couldn't." He tightened his arms around her, and she leaned back into his embrace.

"Did you really know, the moment you saw me?"

"Absolutely."

She leaned her head against his shoulder, then whispered, "I never stopped loving you, Joe."

He kissed her temple, his arms still around her. "It'd be easier for me to stop breathing. I just think of you as...a part of me. I know it doesn't sound all that romantic—"

"It's very romantic."

The rain was almost upon them, and a few drops splashed them as they hurried inside the sliding glass door. Once inside, they watched the water sheeting down, listened for the thunder, counted to seven and looked up in the sky to see lightning slash through the heavens, illuminating the early-evening sky.

She leaned back against him as his hands slid up beneath the oversize sweatshirt, then she struggled out of it. Her shorts and panties soon joined his clothing on the floor, and they stretched out in front of the glass door overlooking the storm.

"That violent," she whispered. "That quick. I knew the moment I saw you that you were going to be important to me."

He ran one of his hands up and down her back, touching her, soothing her. He'd grabbed one of the large quilts from their bed, and now they lay wrapped inside it, still watching the storm.

"I almost followed you back to your room and asked you out to lunch. I had to force myself to wait for dinner."

"I would've gone out with you then. Right away."

"I couldn't believe it when you asked me in—"

She mock-punched his arm. "Don't remind me!"

"I was flattered."

"I was stupid."

"No, you weren't. You just knew what you wanted."

"I wanted to feel something." She kissed the slight dark stubble on his chin. "I didn't want to stay all frozen and tied up inside."

"That's funny, because I thought of you that way."

"What way?"

"Like an ice princess." He kissed her back. "But I always knew you had a lot of emotion locked up inside. I just hoped you'd give it to me."

"You've got it," she whispered, feeling safe in the circle of his arms. "All of me."

THEY CONTINUED to refine both treatment and pitch, but now it was simply a matter of getting a handle on their nerves and waiting for the big day.

Their appointment was for five days from now. They planned on driving into the city the day before and spending the night in a hotel, so there would be less to worry about on the actual day. They could sleep in or not, but they'd be near enough to the studio that they couldn't possibly be late for their afternoon appointment.

Now, as Joe had said so many times before, it was simply a matter of distracting themselves.

They played tennis and swam, went to the Palm Springs library on Sunrise Way and read all the current magazines, watched CNN, shopped at Jensen's Market for gourmet treats and helped Sam cook up incredibly fun cuisine.

They sat out in the hot tub at night and enjoyed the stars in the cold night sky. Nina enjoyed running up her charge cards at some of the more expensive shops in the desert, and Joe continually tinkered on his car.

They made a pact not to change another thing in the treatment, because rewrites could spiral out of control and suck the life out of a story so fast it wasn't funny.

Nina gardened, helping Sam and several staff members maintain the flawless grounds. She'd always believed in having a special object of contemplation and worship, and for her it was the garden.

Covered with sunscreen and wearing long sleeves and a huge straw hat, she worked with the plants, digging her fingers into the rich soil and watering the exotic vegetation. Parrots screamed in the palm trees above, and she remembered that Robert's third wife had had a thing for exotic birds. When they'd divorced, the actor had simply let them loose.

But the joke had been on him, for the three birds had decided to hang around, and now made his life miserable. What had once been a quietly idyllic plot of land was now their home, and raucous cries, shrieks and caustic comments filled the air above their heads.

The wind was blowing today, the weather crisp and clear. She and Joe laughed at Stan's attempts to catch a hummingbird, brought to the most fragrant part of the garden by the elaborate hummingbird feeders.

They looked like bright, tiny jewels, furiously beating their wings and hovering practically motionless in the dry desert air.

"They're not supposed to be able to do that, you know," Joe said. He was helping her repot several kitchen herbs, and handed her a small clump of lemon basil. "Or maybe it was the bumblebee."

"It's funny how much you can do if you don't know you're not supposed to be able to do it," she said, taking the tiny plant and potting it, pressing earth firmly around its roots. "I wonder if we would've even tried if we'd known the odds."

"You want it bad enough, you don't even think about stuff like that."

She knew what he meant. Nina didn't want to dwell on what might happen to them once they arrived at the studio. She knew she could possibly be meeting up with some of the same people who had absolute contempt for her and the idea of her even having a career. They'd believed she was Joe's plaything, that she dabbled in writing while he did the real work.

She was beautiful, and female, and both qualities had worked against her.

Their response was based in fear, she knew that now. But the memories were still painful, and she wondered how things would stand between them once this particular pitch was over.

Most of the time it was too much to think about, thus she pushed it out of her mind and determined to live in the moment. With Joe.

HE TOOK HER to dinner at one of the desert's fanciest resort hotels the night before they left for Los Angeles. Dinner and dancing would be a surefire distraction. They both needed it.

He could sense her nervousness building, and it wasn't helping his own emotional state.

Now, sitting across from her at a candlelit table, he was glad he'd thought to get them out of the house. They still had to pack, and that would take up the remainder of the evening. Once they were on the road, both of them would be less nervous.

It was always the waiting that killed you.

She looked beautiful tonight, and so much healthier than when he'd first seen her. He'd always liked the way she put herself together, and tonight was no exception.

An outfit most women referred to as a little black dress, only on his wife it was stunning. Sort of like a glittery tank top that ended well above the knee. Black stockings and high, high heels. Her hair was swept up into some sort of style, he wasn't sure what it was called, and diamond earrings winked in her ears.

She'd given him back her wedding ring at the Malibu house the night she'd left. He'd been self-conscious about the tiny stone he'd bought for her when they'd first married, and once they'd started to make decent money, he'd replaced it. Now, that same diamond felt as if it were burning a hole in his pocket.

Maybe he was rushing her, but he didn't think so.

He'd picked this particular hotel with care, as he knew there was a band, and a good one. They'd always loved to dance together, and it was as good a way as any to release tension.

Distraction. The name of the game was distraction.

Over coffee and dessert, he wondered how he'd managed to get so lucky.

"Here's to second chances," he said, picking up his flute of champagne.

"Second chances," she murmured, then touched the rim of her glass to his.

"I don't want you to worry, Nina. I'm not going to let anything bad happen."

She'd taken a sip of her champagne, but now she set it down with a sigh. "I know Joe." She wondered if he would agree to doing the pitch alone, and tried to think of a way to convince him.

"Nope. Not an option."

She glanced away from him, frustrated at how easily he had always been able to read her.

"It's a good story, Joe."

"It *is* a great story. But that's not the point." It was the most perfect of openings, and he took it, reaching into his pocket and taking out the small jeweler's ring box. He slid it across the table before she could say another word, and simply waited.

She hesitated, and he knew he'd surprised her. Then, her movements tentative, she opened it and stared at the ring that, so many months ago, had never been off her finger.

"You kept it." The words were blurted out, and he smiled.

"Yeah."

"I thought you might have sold it."

"Well, I thought about doing something dramatic like throwing it into the ocean, but there wasn't any big gesture in the world that would have made me feel better at the time."

"Does this mean—"

"Yep."

"You're sure."

"You bet."

She looked across the small table, straight at him, her eyes glistening, then circled his wrist gently with her fingers.

"I still have the first ring."

That touched him more than anything else she might have said.

"Joe, you could probably find someone who's—"

"A lot less trouble. I know." They couldn't take their eyes off each other, and he knew she was remembering that same afternoon, when he'd proposed and she'd finally accepted.

"Well." She cleared her throat and took the ring out of its plush box. She glanced back at him as he took it from her and slipped it on her finger. "You realize this means you're getting involved with your 'bitch of an ex-wife.'"

"I'm sorry about that one. You caught me off guard."

She smiled, then reached for his face, cupped his chin in her hand.

"I'm not going to lose you over this. It's not worth it."

He narrowed his eyes, seeing what was coming and not liking it.

"Nina, don't try to pull anything before we see how it goes. Things change. People change. You may not know it, but you like more of the business than you think. You've always liked pitching stories."

She didn't say anything, and he decided to forestall any argument. They couldn't risk moving apart when they had to present a united front.

"Humor me," he said.

"How?"

He had her attention now.

"Just something I used to fantasize about when we were living in Hollywood."

"Tell me."

"I thought about—having children. And about how we'd start a family. I wanted to make enough money to take you on a second honeymoon, anywhere in the world you wanted to go."

He knew she'd already seen much of the world, much more than he had. Now she leaned forward, her attention caught.

"Where would you want to go?" she asked.

"Paris."

"Oh, I love that city."

"Paris. I dreamed about taking you to one of the most expensive hotels, and carrying you into a suite that overlooked the city."

Her green eyes were lit with excitement, and he continued his fantasy.

"The bed would be covered with flowers. We'd stay there two weeks, make love every night, get you pregnant—"

The quick sheen of tears in her eyes stopped him.

"Nina?"

"Oh, Joe, I've been such a coward."

"No."

"Let's do it, as soon as I feel better."

"As soon as the doctor gives us the go-ahead."

She laughed then, through her tears, and reached for his hand. "It kind of brings a whole new meaning to the phrase, 'We'll always have Paris.'"

Casablanca. One of her favorite movies. He'd given her the tape their first Christmas together, and they'd watched it every couple of months or so. And always on New Year's Eve.

He squeezed her fingers in his.

"I always knew, even as a kid, that when Bogie said, 'Here's looking at you, kid,' what he was really telling her was that he loved her."

"Oh, I know. It kills me every time, how it ends, but it couldn't have happened any other way."

"He had to let her go."

The band started playing, and music drifted toward them. They were still holding hands as Joe stood up.

"Feel like dancing?"

She smiled up at him, then stood, draped her arms around his neck and kissed him with such sweetness it almost made his heart stop beating.

"I think," she whispered, her lips a fraction from his, "this is the beginning of a beautiful friendship."

Chapter Ten

They packed that same evening.

Sam brought in their clean laundry, and Nina dragged two duffel bags out of the closet. She usually packed for both of them, and Joe saw no reason to upset her by changing the way they'd always done things.

They were only going to be gone for a day, so it wasn't as if they needed an extensive wardrobe.

Nina decided to go with a very classic, formal, glacial look. Expensive black slacks. A cashmere sweater of the same color. People associated black with artists, and she'd play along with that particular fantasy.

She packed makeup carefully, selecting just the right shades to offset the pallor of her skin.

Joe, she knew from past experience, would blaze into the studio office in jeans and a black T-shirt. He hated the world of suits, felt strangled wearing a tie and wore both as infrequently as possible.

Once their bags were packed and against the far wall, she went straight to bed. Joe had wandered out into the kitchen earlier, but now she wasn't sure where he was.

He'd wake her if he needed her.

She studied the brilliant diamond in her second wedding ring. It flashed fire in the light from the bedside lamp, and she twisted the ring slightly on her finger.

It felt right. Like coming home. She reached up and switched off the light, then burrowed beneath the covers.

Tomorrow, and all its problems, would be here soon enough.

HE WAS in the kitchen, talking to Arnie.

"So don't get worried if I do anything out of the ordinary. It's a great story, Arn, we can take it to another studio if those bastards try anything with Nina."

"I'm with you." The greatest thing about having Arnie for an agent was that because he'd been around for such a long time, he was absolutely un-flappable. Nothing fazed him.

Though what Joe planned to do at the studio two days from now just might.

"I think you've hit on a very deep truth, Joe. She may have to go through this in order to... integrate the entire experience."

"They may give her some trouble. Oh, nothing we could call them on, I know how these guys operate. But I just wanted you to know, I'm not throwing over the entire project. But if these guys want this script, they have to come clean about both of us writing it. They have to respect her contribution to the work."

He could almost hear Arnie's smile over the phone.

"And other than work, how are things going?"

"I owe you one. We went out to dinner tonight and I gave her back her wedding ring."

"She took it?"

"It's on her finger as we speak."

"I'm delighted for both of you. Have you set a date?"

Briefly, he told his friend about the divorce papers he'd never bothered to sign.

Arnie sighed, then started to laugh. "I'm getting on in years. Do an old man a favor, and forget to tell her that little detail until *after* the pitch."

HE SAT out by the pool for almost an hour after talking to Arnie, and thought of all the ways the game was played.

They'd offered him one of the most beautiful actresses in film history, a chance to have sex with a goddess, in exchange for dumping Nina.

He hadn't taken the bait.

They'd tried to convince him of all the money he'd earn if he didn't have to split it with another person.

He hadn't listened.

They'd told him flat out she was dragging him down, and he'd told them all to go to hell. Not the quickest way to success, but a path he could live with.

The final confrontation had occurred at Robert's Malibu beach house. He'd lived a few doors down from them, they'd gotten it into their heads they'd buy a house on the beach, but had been renting with the option to buy.

That house had so many unhappy memories, he doubted he ever wanted to see it again.

He and Nina had been working on a new script in the series, but tensions had been pulling them apart. The work wasn't going well, but he'd hidden the fact that afternoon when he'd arrived at Robert's for a barbecue.

Nina hadn't been invited.

This was no ordinary barbecue, no pleasant cookout on a sunny day. It had been a summons. And Joe disliked being at anyone's beck and call.

Robert Corbin really hadn't been at fault. The actor hadn't cared who worked on the script or how it was done, as long as it was on the page by the time shooting started. He was driven by the purest of egos, and only cared about how he was affected. This way of thinking might have accounted for the fact that he was on his fifth marriage.

But two of the producers, big studio people who were responsible for the financing of the film, just had it in their heads that Joe was the brains behind the operation.

He'd gotten a beer from the houseboy, then walked out onto the deck. It hurt him, to think of Nina just a few doors away, being shut out and ignored. Knowing Nina's past the way he did, he never wanted her to be silenced again.

The pressure to give in was relentless.

It started before he'd even finished that first beer, and continued through the appetizer and main meal. He was halfway through his steak and it could have been compressed sawdust for all the enjoyment he was deriving from it. They'd pushed and pushed and pushed, and he'd finally shoved his plate away and put down his fork.

"Find someone else," he'd said, his temper firmly in check.

"Now, Joseph, there's certainly no need to get testy over such a simple matter."

"It's not that simple."

"I think it is." Michael Carson, one of the producers and head of Wolfmoon Productions, smiled that smile Joe couldn't stomach. "Whatever kind of hold she has over you, I think you should seriously consider breaking off the relationship. It's hurting you, Joseph, and you can't afford to be hurt for long in this town."

The devil came into your life in many guises, with so many temptations. Joe thought of how many people before him had sold their souls.

He couldn't be one of them. After exploding onto the scene with brilliant work, they'd slowly been ground down until they simply churned out studio fodder.

What the hell did I get in this for? he thought, and his gaze went to the house three houses down. Nina. He thought about picking up the cellular phone on the dining table and giving her a call, telling her that none of it was worth it if you couldn't even call the work your own.

He wasn't naive. Business was business. But this was above and beyond the necessary compromises any creative person had to make. Cutting Nina loose wasn't any sort of compromise, it would be like severing his arm from his body.

Or cutting out his own heart.

He set his beer down, and directed his attention to Michael Carson. The man was like so many others in Hollywood, basically a gutless wonder who hid his fear of women with games, intimidation and outright ruthless behavior if the situation demanded it.

"I've got a news flash for you, Michael. I write, she writes. She goes, I go. It's as simple as that."

The producer's cold, gray eyes had iced over, and Joe knew they'd reached the critical moment. He felt as if he were back in the ring, fighting with bare fists, no-holds-barred and every nerve in his body poised. Waiting for the attack.

Moving in for the kill.

The studio head merely stared at him, and Joe pushed his deck chair back, got up and started toward the sliding glass doors.

"Joseph."

He stopped. But he didn't turn around. He could feel Michael right behind him. Too close. One male animal challenging another.

"Why did you turn down Julia Powell?" Joe could hear the smile in his voice. The easy, phony smile designed to fool him into thinking they had any sort of relationship, any sort of kinship. "I mean, it's common knowledge she'll make any guy happy."

Joe shook his head, amazed. They might be wearing expensive designer sportsclothes, and buy sunglasses whose cost would feed a family in his old neighborhood for two weeks. But underneath it all, Michael's type were all the same. Insecure guys out for a thrill.

Joe cut right to the heart of it. "I'm a married man."

Michael laughed. "What says that has to stop you?"

"Save it." He turned back toward the door and started away from the men.

"You're truly a piece of work, Joseph. She must be something if all she has to do is twitch her sweet little fanny and you come running."

Without missing a beat, Joe turned, and put everything he had into a solid punch that hit Michael Carson squarely in his surgically altered face. The man fell back on to a filled buffet table, onto the food, then slid slowly down until he dropped to the deck, unconscious.

Utter silence. Complete and utter silence.

He turned to the others, gave them all the benefit of one long, last look. And he felt free in a way he hadn't in the longest time.

"Well," he said, rubbing his fist, "I guess this means I'm off the picture."

HE'D ARRIVED back home to find her packing.

"What is this?" He took a pile of her clothing and threw it across the room. He'd been geared up for a fight and only gotten one punch in. Now, to come home and find the woman he loved running from him was more than he could endure.

"Get out of my way, Joe." Nina was serious about this, whipping around their bedroom like a madwoman, dumping clothing, cosmetics and books into two huge suitcases.

"Why are you doing this?"

"I should have done it long ago, Joe." She stopped the frenzied activity for a moment and looked him squarely in the eye. "I don't want to see the type of people Michael Carson hires doing a John Blackheart script. I love that character, and he deserves better. So if it means you do it alone—"

"No, you don't! Nina, I just—"

She slammed one suitcase shut and hauled it off the bed.

"Nina, will you listen—"

She was bumping the two cases down the stairs, and he saw the full extent of her fury in that she finally let them go and they fell, crashing down the stairs and into the small foyer.

He'd left her alone too long. Too many nights. She was out of control and he couldn't stop her.

He followed her out to her car, the gray Mercedes Robert had bought her in a fit of gratitude. And watched as she threw one suitcase in the trunk, the other in the back seat.

When she turned back toward him, she was twisting her diamond wedding ring off her finger. Tears were running down her face, and he stepped forward, closed his hands over her shoulders.

She jerked back as if he'd burned her.

"No, don't stop me." She choked on a sob as she threw the ring at him. "I can't do this anymore."

She got into the car, gunned the engine, and squealed out onto the highway with a spattering of gravel.

He must have picked up the ring before he went inside. He must have, because when he finally unclenched his fist, he was holding it.

And his palm was bleeding.

THE ONLY THING he was thankful for, Joe thought as he stared up into the desert night sky, was that this time Michael Carson wouldn't be at the pitch meeting. He wasn't sure he could have been civil to the man.

He glanced toward the house as he heard a noise, then saw Nina walking toward him.

"Couldn't sleep?" she called out softly.

He nodded, then patted the cushion beside him. The wicker sofa was positioned so it afforded a person the most beautiful view of the valley below. Lights were winking out, and soon everything would be in darkness.

She sat down next to him, and laid her head on his shoulder.

"What are you thinking?" she said.

"I was remembering."

"What?"

"How good it felt to punch Michael Carson."

She laughed, then snuggled closer.

"I heard about that after I left. From the guy who used to do my hair."

"It never did make the papers."

"He never tried to sue?"

"Over what? A bloody nose? I didn't try to kill him, I just wanted to shut him up."

They sat in a companionable silence for a while, looking at the night sky. The wind was blowing fiercely tonight, but as both of them had sweaters on, they didn't feel too cold.

"No matter what happens, I'm going to keep thinking of Paris," she said.

His arm was around her, and he pulled her close.

"Whatever happens, we're in it together. I want you to promise me one thing, Nina."

"What?"

"No matter what happens, I want you to trust me."

She looked up into his eyes, and he saw a contentment in her expression that hadn't been there in the longest time.

"I do."

THEY HIT the road the following morning.

Nina had a little trouble leaving, even though Sam assured her countless times that he would remember Ollie's daily ration of Q-Tips and would carefully measure Henry's food. Stan and Clyde had been curled up together, sleeping on the kitchen floor in a bright spot of sunshine.

And Joe couldn't help smiling, because it was just the way his wife was.

"Nina, we're going away for a day, not weeks."

"Oh, I know, but—"

He finally got her into the car and they started down the hill.

It was a gray day, drizzly and overcast. He'd nagged her into wearing a sweater, and the bright red pullover seemed to give her face a little more color.

He cranked the heater up on high and turned the radio to a jazz station.

They were on their way. No turning back now.

They hadn't gone more than twenty miles when the car started to falter.

"What's wrong?" Nina asked, as an ominous pinging noise sounded from beneath the hood.

"Damn!"

"Oh, Joe, you didn't—"

"Don't even say it." He'd thought he'd put the car back together properly after his tinkering around with it, gathering research for the Blackheart screenplay.

But he'd obviously done something wrong.

He pulled over to the side of the interstate, well off the road. They sat in silence for a moment, then he reached over and took her hand.

"Thanks for not saying it."

She picked up the car phone. "We can give Sam a call, maybe he can bring my car out. Then we can take him home and start all over again."

"Good plan."

But Sam wasn't home.

"He said he was going out for groceries. Wasn't that it? I guess we could wait here for a while...." Nina bit her lip as she studied the phone in her hands.

"Do we know anyone else?"

"I'll call Diane."

But the salon was closed, and all she got was her friend's answering machine.

"Great." Joe rubbed the bridge of his nose. "Great. The perfect start to a perfect pitch."

"Okay. Hang on. Let's not panic."

"We could rent a car."

"Where?" The interstate cut through the desert, and except for typical truck stops, there wasn't much else in sight for miles.

"Right. Well, I guess I'd better call for a tow." Joe called information and wrote down several numbers. After being told for the third time that the company's tow truck was out and it would be at least another couple of hours before they could get to their car, he hung up the phone and stared at Nina.

Now he felt like a total fool.

Nina looked cold, so he turned the ignition on. At least they could have a little heat.

But it seemed something had happened to the battery, and he got absolutely nothing.

"Hang on," he told his wife, then jumped out of the Mercedes, slamming the door behind him. He walked out closer to the highway and stuck out his thumb, in the universal gesture that meant asking for a ride.

Several cars passed him before he felt a light tap on his shoulder.

"Joe, get back in the car, you've got to be freezing!"

"Nina, get inside. I'll find us a ride sooner or later."

"This is insane—"

"Get in the car!"

She obeyed, but not without glaring at him first.

He must have looked pretty angry, because no one bothered to stop. Almost half an hour later, he saw Nina get back out of the car. She'd taken off her sweater, and merely wore her black leather jacket over a red T-shirt and jeans. She ran to his side and grabbed his arm.

"Let's think this through."

"Nina, I'm not in the mood."

"You look like some kind of serial killer! No one's going to stop for you. Now, I've got a plan...."

HE HID behind the car. She took off her jacket and stood by the road—thrusting out her chest along with her thumb.

The third car that passed, a white Ford truck, squealed to a stop.

Joe caught up with her as she ran to the passenger side door.

The guy inside looked like a walking, breathing advertisement for a north woods beer commercial. Heavyset, with a bushy brown beard and twinkling brown eyes, dressed in a plaid shirt and faded jeans, Larry Cudahay was only too happy to help.

"What's a little girl like you doing out on a morning like this?" he boomed out. His face fell when he saw Joe, but he accepted masculine defeat graciously and agreed to drive them to the nearest truck stop.

He was a curious man, and asked them what they were up to. When he found out they wrote screenplays, his day was complete.

"*Deadly Threat?* With John Blackheart? Oh, man, that was a *great* picture! I saw it five times. You know, I especially liked the part where the diesel truck ran off the cliff and blew up...."

He stayed with them at the truck stop as Joe called several other towing services. And had just as little luck as before.

"Now, let me get this straight," Larry said, chewing on a piece of beef jerky, a bottle of Squirt in his other fist. "You've got to be in Hollywood tomorrow afternoon, or I never get to see another good John Blackheart movie, is that it?"

"That about sums it up," Nina replied.

"Oh, man, you guys *have* to make it there! That last one, where they divorced and then his wife was killed? I walked out! And I like a girl with a good set a' hooters, but she just wasn't the type of woman that John would have taken up with, know what I mean?"

Joe nodded his head, studying the burly man, and wondering how they could incorporate him into the movie. He was too good a character. Well, didn't Weather Mountain have to have mechanics? Maintenance men?

"What would you normally be doing today, Larry?" Nina asked.

"It's my day off. I was just going to get some material to fix my back fence."

Joe thought for a second, then said, "How much would it cost us to hire you to drive us to Riverside?"

Larry's eyes lit up. "I'd do it for free if I knew John Blackheart was going to be back up on that screen. You know, I've been meaning to ask, in the second one, how did that guy do that fall off the skyscraper? My son wondered about that one—"

"How about gas and a hundred bucks an hour?" Joe offered.

Larry's eyes bulged out of his head, and he practically choked on the piece of jerky he was chewing.

"Hell, let's go!"

THEY STOPPED at a pancake house for breakfast, and Larry insisted it was his treat. He was absolutely thrilled to be this close to the movie business, and Joe thought of how innocent he'd once been. Movies were wonderful. Good always triumphed.

It had been a long time since he'd thought that way.

While they drank one last cup of coffee, Nina slipped away to the bathroom. And Joe studied Larry, and decided to ask him a question.

"Can I ask you something, Larry?"

"Sure. Fire away."

"Do you think women are as capable as men are?"

"In what way?"

"Well—writing movies, for example."

"Hmm." He regarded Joe closely. "Why are you asking me this?"

Briefly, his eye on the direction Nina had gone, Joe told him.

"Hell, that's what made those first three Blackheart movies so damn good, if you ask me. You guys work real good together, but it was the relationship John had with his wife that impressed me. He was a real gentleman."

Joe caught sight of Nina, making her way back to their table.

"Thanks, Larry. I appreciate it. More than you'll ever know."

BY THE TIME they were halfway to Riverside, Larry had pitched them his script. Nina wrote him a list of how-to books and took his address and phone number.

"When we get back to the compound, we'll invite you up for dinner one night. You and your little boy."

Larry was a single father, struggling to raise an eleven-year-old son.

"And if our script is accepted, I'm sure we can get you a couple of tickets to the premiere."

Larry dropped them off at the Riverside Greyhound station, and went inside with them. There was a bus leaving for Los Angeles within twenty minutes, and Joe purchased them tickets. Then he walked across the street to an ATM and got out enough money to pay Larry, with a bonus besides.

"Aw, this is too much," he began, but Joe silenced him.

"We would have been really stuck without you, Larry. Neither of us will forget what you did."

Nina leaned over and kissed the burly man on his weathered cheek. "Thanks, Larry. I guess guardian angels come in all shapes and sizes."

The man actually blushed, then cleared his throat. "I'm no angel, ma'am. When I saw you standing out on that road—" He glanced at Joe. "Well, maybe I'll just leave it at that."

THEY SAT in the back of the bus, stashing their duffel bags beneath their seats. The bus started up, with a grinding of gears, and Nina snuggled back into Joe's embrace.

"Just think, if you hadn't fixed your car, none of this would have happened."

He sighed. "I like the way you think."

The bus lumbered through the city, then reached the highway and began to pick up speed.

"I think we met Larry for a reason," Nina said.

"How's that?"

"The way he loved John. And his adventures. That's who we're writing for, Joe, not the suits at the studios."

"I know what you mean."

She leaned into him, then whispered, "I can do it, Joe. I know I can. No matter how bad it gets, all I'll have to do is think of Larry." Then she kissed him.

He snuck his hands up the back of her sweater. The bus was practically empty, with only a few other passengers up front.

"I was thinking of another type of distraction," he whispered, then kissed her again.

"It would certainly make the trip more entertaining."

He fingered the fastening of her bra. "Time flies when you're having fun."

She laughed. "I like your style, Morrissey."

Chapter Eleven

They arrived at the downtown Los Angeles bus station by late afternoon, and found a cabdriver outside who drove them to the Beverly Hills Hotel. Large, imposing and pink, the huge luxury hotel was a landmark on Sunset Boulevard. Joe hadn't really planned on staying there, but he decided that after the day they'd had, they both deserved a little pampering.

Once inside, they simply shed their damp clothing and headed for a hot tub in the huge bathroom. Nina used up almost all of the perfumed bath gel, pouring it under the water as the marble tub was filled to the brim. Then she and Joe got carefully in, trying not to slosh water all over the place.

Using the bathroom phone, he called room service.

"Chicken wings or *fajitas?*" he asked as Nina lay stretched out in the tub, luxuriating in the warmth and silkiness of the water.

"Both."

They ate in front of the fire, wrapped in the robes they found on the back of the bathroom door. And later, curled up in bed, they talked.

"Let's make a pact," Nina said.

"About?"

"Well, it's just that I think we work so much better as a team."

"You won't find me arguing with that." He could tell she was nervous about tomorrow afternoon, and he could empathize. It had been almost three years since she'd pitched a story to a studio, and the last time she'd participated, her contribution hadn't exactly been wanted.

"So, we're a package deal?"

He kissed her. "That's the way it goes down. And I don't want you trying any of that noble stuff, like running away for my own good."

She shook her head. Her blond hair, silky and clean from their bath, fell over her bare shoulders. He had to resist the desire to grab a handful of it and ease her down on the bed. She looked tired. As much fun as their day had been, it was still an exhausting way to travel.

"Okay." She looked so relieved, and he just couldn't resist. He'd be gentle with her, he'd do all the work, but he couldn't lie in bed with her and not make love to her.

"Joe!" She smiled up at him as he rolled over and pinned her to the soft mattress.

He kissed her once, twice, three times.

"Joe." Her voice had softened now, her body an erotic example of total feminine submission.

"I can't help it," he whispered. "I'm crazy about your team spirit."

HE GOT UP EARLY the following morning, and phoned for some coffee. He'd never liked sleeping in strange beds, and whether in a hammock or a five-star hotel, he was never completely comfortable.

Now, before his breakfast of caffeine and sugar arrived, he studied his sleeping wife. And wished he could tell her half the things in his mind, in his heart. They were so easy to write down on paper, compared to speaking them aloud.

When I think of how my life was before you...

There had been an emptiness inside him for a long time, a loneliness, a feeling of not quite being complete. He'd moved to the studio apartment in Hollywood with little more than his dreams, then looked up to see an angel standing in his doorway.

Not a typical angel. This one had determined green eyes and a stubborn little chin. And passion. Even when she'd tried to hide it from him, he'd known it was there.

She slept so soundly, barely moved. Except for the gentle rise and fall of her chest, he'd barely know she was alive. But her breathing was easier than it had been last night, and he was grateful for that.

I had no idea what real happiness was, until I met you.

That she had invited him back to her room after their first dinner together had struck him as a miracle, a gift from the gods. That she'd slowly let him into her heart and shared her deepest secrets and dreams with him made him realize that this type of closeness with this woman he loved was what he'd waited all his life for.

Fighting had been so easy. Getting into that ring and risking serious bodily injury had never frightened him as much as loving Nina.

Emotions had been what had scared him to death.

And he'd been full of them. He'd never felt he was good enough for her, not during all the years they were married. And he'd made some emotional mistakes he'd paid for, leaving her alone while he tried to put together the next deal, the next job that would make her proud of him.

She'd always been proud of him, he knew that now.

You give meaning to everything I do. That's why all of it happened, why I did it. I wanted to give it back to you.

Their bond went beyond that of lovers or spouses. They shared a passion, a vision, and when hers had been silenced, he'd hurt for her. More than she would probably ever know.

He'd been silenced in other ways. By the absence of a father. By poverty. By the neighborhood.

And once outside it all, he'd wanted to do something with his life. Make his time on earth matter.

He'd always made up stories in his head. Books had meant more to him than anyone suspected. He could pretend he was the hero within their pages, and everything would turn out all right in the end.

He'd made enough money to ensure some of those dreams came true. He'd finally moved his mother out of her house in Hollywood, and she'd settled in Puerto Rico with two of her sisters. He'd have to call her soon. She'd been so upset when Nina had left, and never stopped praying the two of them would find each other again.

She had photos of both of them in her bible, along with one of their wedding pictures. And she told him she burned a white candle each night, hoping for a miracle.

It had happened. Between his mother's faith and Arnie's meddling, they'd been given a second chance. It was more than most people got.

Nina was like a vital organ he couldn't survive without. He hadn't been exaggerating the situation in his mind that day on Robert's deck. Cutting her loose from their writing partnership, cutting her out of his life would have been as painful as losing an arm or leg.

She stirred in her sleep, and he continued to study her.

I want to give you everything. Only the best, for you, for our children, for the world I want to create with you.

It had been hard to compete against a trust fund the size of Nina's, but he understood now that he'd been wrong. She'd brought it to their marriage like an old-fashioned dowry, to be used by both of them. He had rejected it, and in the process, rejected her.

Silenced her in another way.

She was a fighter, his wife. Her looks often fooled people, they expected the typical, fragile, feminine blonde. Nina broke every stereotype, she came into the ring fighting, passionate, ready to do battle. Each time she'd been knocked down, she came back up swinging.

A true champion.

She'd instinctively known the importance of dreams, just as he had. And though they'd come from opposite ends of the world and from two families that couldn't have been more dissimilar, they'd recognized each other as soon as they'd met.

Because they'd both decided to take a path that was just a little off the beaten track.

Once they'd joined forces, they'd been unbeatable.

Once they'd split up, nothing else mattered.

The world was a crazy place, and happy endings were never part of the guarantee. Somehow, he'd been given a second chance at life, an opportunity to cast off the life he'd been living, the half-dead existence, the depression that had dogged him every day of his life since she'd left him.

He'd opened his eyes each morning and wondered why he was even making an attempt to go on.

Now, with Nina back in his life, he didn't even want to sleep, there was so much living yet to be done.

The soft knock at the door broke into his thoughts, and Joe went to answer it.

Within minutes, he'd poured himself a cup of coffee and was scanning the paper.

He'd let her sleep. With the day they had ahead of them, she'd need it. He'd called Arnie the minute they'd arrived at the hotel. The agent knew where they were and what had happened.

Before the day was over, everything would be settled. During one of the desert nights he'd sat and scrutinized the stars, he'd made up his mind about what he was going to do.

Heroes might only exist in the world of fiction. He might be better at writing them than actually trying anything himself. But today he was going to do things a little differently.

Today, he wouldn't make the wrong decision.

Today, he would be her hero.

PARAMOUNT STUDIOS WAS on Melrose Avenue. Joe had always liked it for a rather peculiar reason. In the old movies, and in Three Stooges episodes, whenever they'd needed to show a movie studio, they'd filmed Paramount's famous gates.

Now they guided their rental car through those gates, smiled at the young man working the guardhouse, took the pass he gave them and continued inside the studio grounds.

They parked, then, following directions the guard had given them, started toward the offices where they would pitch their project.

It was so familiar, like an actor's audition. Find the office, say hello to the secretary. Decline the coffee, which was usually pretty bad. And try to stay focused on the work, and not succumb to nerves.

They sat close together on the couch, and he could feel her fear.

"Just remember, they can't even get the project off the ground without a script."

"I know."

"Hey, if all else fails, we'll move to Mexico and write under a different name. Just we keep working together."

She swallowed, then forced a smile. "It feels so strange to be back."

He knew that feeling. And he realized that the mark of a true champion is that he returns to the ring no matter how frightened he is. And keeps getting back up, no matter how many times he falls.

They didn't have to wait long before another secretary came out, this time a young man, and ushered them inside a large conference room.

And seated with the other businessmen around the table was a man from their past.

Michael Carson.

HE WAS HEAD of Titan Productions now, one of the many divisions at the mother studio, Paramount. Joe had read it in the trades the other day. The appointment had been recent, and the man whose nose he'd broken was now considered one of the most powerful people in Hollywood.

He could feel Nina's tension, but he doubted anyone else in the room could. Interestingly enough, there were two women in the room, dressed in black with bright red lipstick. They had that tough, intelligent aura so often found in women who made it this high in a brutal profession.

Stuart Grayson, the head of this particular division within the studio, welcomed them.

"Mr. Carson heard the two of you were working on a script, and asked if he could sit in. I hope that's all right with both of you."

Joe studied his old enemy's face. Even the best plastic surgeon hadn't been able to completely disguise the fact that Michael's nose had been broken. But it actually improved his appearance, giving him less the look of a pretty boy and more the feel of a street fighter.

For one crazy moment, Joe thought of sending him a bill. He smiled at the man, but it didn't reach his eyes. He was in the shark tank now, and knew it.

"It's fine." This was from Nina.

As they sat down across the table from the assembled committee, he whispered, "Remember Paris."

"And Larry," she whispered back.

The usual pleasantries were exchanged, then Stuart leaned forward. He was a basically good man, and had earned a reputation in the business as a man who fought a fair fight.

"I think it's safe to say that none of us enjoyed the last John Blackheart movie. So I hope what you're going to present to us today is a bit more entertaining."

"Without a doubt," Joe said, feeling more confident by the minute. He didn't look at Michael as he began their pitch.

"Nina came up with the basic premise. We've seen skyscrapers, ships, airports, enclosed malls and other areas destroyed in the name of family entertainment. But this one tops them all."

He had a naturally personable tone as he pitched, and stuck with the story. He watched Grayson's reactions, and was gratified to see him lean forward, his intelligent eyes alight with interest.

He moved smoothly into the second act, after convincing the group of producers that they were going to simply ignore the fourth movie in the series and pick up where the third had left off.

He reached the midpoint, and handed it over to Nina.

She began her part of the pitch, and it went smoothly until Michael Carson interrupted.

"Excuse me, could we get some more coffee in here?"

Stuart seemed annoyed, and turned his attention back to Nina.

"Please continue, Mrs. Morrissey." He was an old-fashioned man, uncomfortable with the casual use of first names that was standard in the business.

Nina took a deep breath, and continued. They'd memorized the pitch back in Palm Springs, so she didn't have to refer to the notes spread out in front of them.

She was almost to the end of act two when Michael challenged her.

"Wait a minute, I'm not sure if that will sell. Joe, could you explain it to us a little more clearly?"

JOE FELT cold anger spreading through his body at the way Michael was subtly diminishing Nina. Insulting her. Acting as if she weren't even there.

This time he'd thrown her. She'd been sitting, as neither of them felt comfortable jumping around the room and using all the physical pyrotechnics that were so popular these days. They'd always just come in and told a good story.

He knew her so well, could feel her fear. Memories of the last few times they'd pitched stories flooded him. He hadn't been able to protect her then, but he was sure as hell going to do the job now.

But he couldn't do it for her.

Stuart looked at Nina, caught her eye. "I understood what you were saying, my dear. Please go on. We'll catch Mr. Carson up afterward."

The barb hit home, and Michael sat back in his seat. Joe couldn't be sure, but he thought he might actually be sulking.

Nina didn't respond.

He glanced over at her, and though the room couldn't have been silent for more than a few seconds, to Joe it seemed an eternity.

She cleared her throat. Took a sip from her glass of water.

"Could we have a minute?" Joe asked.

Michael was smiling now, and Joe was determined the bastard wasn't going to win. He had to figure out a way to reach Nina, and reach her fast.

Uncapping one of the black felt-tipped pens that were never far from his side, he scrawled a single line across their notes.

Here's looking at you, kid.

She glanced down, and he saw her expression change, saw that stubborn chin go up, watched as she regained that subtle, emotional strength that had always been such an important part of her personality.

She directed the rest of their pitch straight at Stuart Grayson. He listened as passion filled her voice, as her enthusiasm for the story carried them all to a different place.

She captured their imagination, and the story came alive. They were no longer thinking about the movie, they were seeing it as Nina moved them swiftly from act two into act three, through the final climax and the satisfying resolution. She'd captured them.

One of the women executives smiled, then began to take notes. The other leaned back in her chair, absorbed in thought. Stuart was steepling his fingers in front of him, his elbows resting on the desk.

The only one who didn't look entirely happy was Michael Carson. He was staring at Nina as if he'd never truly seen her before.

Stuart was nodding his head and smiling.

"Very nice. Well thought out. I like the fact that you've given us an authentic John Blackheart movie."

Nothing would be decided right now. Stuart would call Arnie, they would hash out the contract, but Joe was just about certain that they'd sold the studio on making the latest installment of John's adventures.

He still couldn't quite figure out what Michael was doing at their meeting, unless he thought he could talk Stuart out of hiring them to write the screenplay.

But Grayson was a man who made up his own mind. He had a reputation for making good films. When he decided to go ahead with a project, he usually received the studio's full support.

He thanked them for coming in, and told them he would be calling their agent directly.

The minute they reached their rental car, they sped out of the studio gates and found the first pay phone in sight.

"Arnie? Arnie? I think we sold them on it—"

"He's already called me, Joe. Grayson wants the two of you to start work on the screenplay immediately. Normally, I wouldn't want you to do anything until a contract's signed, but I've worked with Stuart before and his word is gold."

"Hang on, tell Nina."

She started to cry as Arnie told her, and watching his wife, Joe realized how much they'd both wanted to do this particular film. They'd created John Blackheart, he was as much a member of their family as if he were one of their children. Now, the final chapter in his story would be told, and it would end the way they'd always envisioned it.

They had coffee and apple strudel at a little Austrian cafe on Melrose, and sat at a table outside enjoying the last of the day's pale, winter sunshine. The slight drizzle had stopped, and the city looked fresh and rain-washed, the hills green in the distance.

"We can drive back to the desert tonight, after rush hour," Nina suggested, cutting into the flaky pastry with her fork.

"You're still worried about the cats, aren't you?"

"Only because they're not used to being alone. Especially Ollie."

"Okay. We have time to see another movie before we leave, if you want."

"Oh, I don't know." She took a sip of her coffee, then leaned toward him, her elbows on the table. And he thought she looked beautiful and elegant, dressed all in black with her light hair shimmering down over her shoulders. "I'd sort of like to just sit and relax."

"Whatever."

"And talk."

"That's fine."

"About . . . wedding plans."

"Oh, God."

He must have looked guilty, because she immediately picked up on it.

"What? Joe, has something happened? Have you—have you changed your mind?"

"No, no, nothing like that, I swear."

"Then what?"

He was silent, desperately trying to put his thoughts in order. Where were the scriptwriters for screenwriters? He could have used some snappy dialogue, something Cary Grant would have said to Kate Hepburn, right about now.

He needed a happy ending.

She was looking at him with such a worried expression in her deep green eyes that he finally just blurted it out.

"I . . . never . . . signed . . . the papers."

"What!"

"I never signed the papers."

"The divorce papers?"

"Right."

She was silent for a few seconds.

"So, then, technically, we've never been divorced."

"Right."

"So we don't have to get remarried."

"No. Not unless you want to, that is." He felt himself fumbling badly. What love did to a man was indescribable. He'd wanted to pick the perfect time and place to tell her, and here they were, in the middle of the street, eating strudel.

"I—I couldn't do it, Nina. I looked at those papers, and I couldn't end it. So I just stuffed them back in another envelope and mailed them to you."

"Oh, Joe."

She was looking at him as if he were some kind of hero.

Her hero.

"That was such a smart thing to do."

"Smartness had nothing to do with it. I just couldn't."

"And I just—"

"Stuffed the letter into your file cabinet without opening it," he finished for her. "I was sort of counting on that. I thought, if we remained married, even if it was only in the eyes of the law, I might have a chance of getting you back."

"You would've come after me?"

"I was getting up my nerve."

''I thought about calling you, the entire time I was driving out to Robert's.''

They simply stared at each other, until Nina said, ''Then we're back to where we started.''

''Oh, no, I think we've gone quite a bit further.'' He cleared his throat so his voice would work. ''I was proud of you in there, Nina. The way you kept going, no matter what he did to you.''

''I couldn't have done it without you.''

''I wouldn't have wanted to be there without you.''

''You know, I realize John Blackheart has just about run his course—''

''Uh-oh.''

''But if he had a son . . .''

As they started to plot, she took out a pen and began taking notes on one of their napkins. He took a sip of his coffee and cut into his strudel, relieved that the worst was over. By the time they finished throwing ideas around, the last bit of daylight had faded and shop lights had come on up and down the busy street.

She surprised him all over again.

''We're married!''

''Yes, Nina. Forever.''

She laughed then, tipping her head back, unable to contain her happiness. It was a sound of such pure, passionate joy that people walking by their table couldn't help smiling.

Epilogue

Arnie Axel wished he was anywhere but Morton's.

The elegant, power restaurant was crowded on this particular Monday night. Anyone who was anyone in the industry commanded a good table.

He had one of the best.

Success didn't really make that much of a difference to Arnie. He'd been at the top, he'd been at the bottom, more times that he could count.

But it was rather gratifying to be successful again.

He was back on top, as a result of *Deadly Threat V: The Final Conflict.* Joe and Nina had completed a brilliant action-adventure screenplay, and the movie had gone on to become the biggest hit of the summer, earning more than any other picture released during that time period. It made three times the money the previous John Blackheart adventure had brought in.

The room came imperceptibly alive, and Arnie knew Robert Corbin had arrived. He watched as the actor of the moment—who had just starred in one of the all-time box office successes in movie history, let alone this past summer—walked into Morton's as if he owned the joint.

He did. For now.

Within minutes, he was at Arnie's table.

He's enjoying all this, Arnie thought, looking at the bronzed skin, the bright blue eyes, the thick, dark hair.

Success. He could smell it. And it was the most powerful aphrodisiac in town.

The girl with him was an up-and-coming actress, a stunning little thing. She hung on Robert's every word, which must have been quite a chore.

Robert ordered them all a round of drinks, then sat back in his chair and grinned at Arnie.

"So, what are Joe and Nina up to these days?"

Robert, Robert. You've got to learn to be more subtle.

"They finished another script and turned it in about two weeks ago."

"Is there a part for me?"

"I'll send you a copy." He didn't dislike Robert, he was simply amazed by the man. It seemed he was one of the few people Arnie knew who actually enjoyed this entire circus. Arnie supported the work, believed in it. The rest of it all simply had to be endured.

"So, how come I never see them at places like this?" Robert asked, playing with a dark curl of the starlet's hair as he spoke.

"They have dinner with me once in a while. But they're not in the country at the moment."

"Huh. Where'd they go?"

"Paris."

"Hey, that's swell. I have to hand it to you, Arnie. You did what no one else in this town could do. You got Joe and Nina together again."

They chatted for a few more minutes, then Robert Corbin moved on with his admiring little entourage, a star shining brightly in his own private universe.

Arnie took another sip of his drink, then glanced around the crowded restaurant and smiled.

Well, he'd managed to get Joe and Nina together again. They'd each written him private letters, thanking him for his little scheme, and he'd been highly gratified at how well things had turned out.

Now they were vacationing in Paris, and if his latest hunch had any validity to it at all, there would be another generation of Morrisseys to contend with in the not-too-distant future.

The room faded away as he thought of his two clients.

If truth were known, he loved them like the children he'd never had. They'd turned to him, both in need of a father figure, as neither had been too lucky with their own.

Father figure. He liked the sound of it.

Grandfather figure. He liked that even better.

He blinked away the sudden moisture that had gathered in his eyes and raised his gin and tonic in a private, heartfelt toast.

"Here's to both of you, Joe and Nina. Wherever you are."

Take 4 bestselling love stories FREE

Plus get a FREE surprise gift!

Special Limited-time Offer

Mail to Harlequin Reader Service®

3010 Walden Avenue
P.O. Box 1867
Buffalo, N.Y. 14269-1867

YES! Please send me 4 free Harlequin American Romance® novels and my free surprise gift. Then send me 4 brand-new novels every month, which I will receive months before they appear in bookstores. Bill me at the low price of $2.71 each plus 25¢ delivery and applicable sales tax, if any.*That's the complete price and—compared to the cover prices of $3.50 each—quite a bargain! I understand that accepting the books and gift places me under no obligation ever to buy any books. I can always return a shipment and cancel at any time. Even if I never buy another book from Harlequin, the 4 free books and the surprise gift are mine to keep forever.

154 BPA AJJF

Name	(PLEASE PRINT)	
Address	Apt. No.	
City	State	Zip

This offer is limited to one order per household and not valid to present Harlequin American Romance® subscribers. *Terms and prices are subject to change without notice. Sales tax applicable in N.Y.

UAM-93R   ©1990 Harlequin Enterprises Limited

HARLEQUIN®

A M E R I C A N ◆ R O M A N C E®

Once in a while, there's a man so special, a story so different, that your pulse races, your blood rushes. We call this

AMERICAN ROMANCE heartbeat

Gabriel Falconi is one such man, and FALLING ANGEL is one such book. Two years after his death, Gabriel is back on earth. He's still drop-dead handsome with his long black hair. But this time he's here to right three wrongs he'd done in his earthly life. Will this fallen angel earn his wings?

FALLING ANGEL
by

Anne Stuart

Don't miss the first of these sexy, special heroes. They'll make your HEARTBEAT!

Available in December wherever Harlequin books are sold. Watch for more Heartbeat stories, coming your way soon!

HEART

1993 Keepsake

CHRISTMAS

Stories

Capture the spirit and romance of Christmas with KEEPSAKE CHRISTMAS STORIES, a collection of three stories by favorite historical authors. The perfect Christmas gift!

Don't miss these heartwarming stories, available in November wherever Harlequin books are sold:

ONCE UPON A CHRISTMAS by Curtiss Ann Matlock
A FAIRYTALE SEASON by Marianne Willman
TIDINGS OF JOY by Victoria Pade

ADD A TOUCH OF ROMANCE TO YOUR HOLIDAY SEASON WITH KEEPSAKE CHRISTMAS STORIES!

HX93

When the only time you have for yourself is...

STOLEN *moments* ™

Christmas is such a busy time—with shopping, decorating, writing cards, trimming trees, wrapping gifts....

When you do have a few *stolen moments* to call your own, treat yourself to a brand-new *short* novel. Relax with one of our Stocking Stuffers— or with all six!

Each STOLEN MOMENTS title is a complete and original contemporary romance that's the perfect length for the busy woman of the nineties! Especially at Christmas...

And they make perfect **stocking stuffers**, too! (For your mother, grandmother, daughters, friends, co-workers, neighbors, aunts, cousins—all the other women in your life!)

Look for the STOLEN MOMENTS display in December

STOCKING STUFFERS:

HIS MISTRESS Carrie Alexander
DANIEL'S DECEPTION Marie DeWitt
SNOW ANGEL Isolde Evans
THE FAMILY MAN Danielle Kelly
THE LONE WOLF Ellen Rogers
MONTANA CHRISTMAS Lynn Russell

HSM2

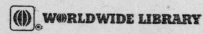 **WORLDWIDE LIBRARY**